Bakery Wars

By Hannah Willow

ISBN eBook: 978-1-959981-77-0
ISBN paperback: 978-1-959981-78-7

Editor: Fe Foster
Developmental Editor: Angela Grimes
Cover Art: Getcovers.com
Formatting: Huckleberry Rahr

Books in

Small Town Love, Sass, and Gossip

Book 1: Bakery Wars

Book 2: Playing It Queer

Book 3: Booked For Love

Books By Hannah Willow

Love in Golden Creek
> Book 1: The Rancher's Envoy
> Book 2: The Ranch Hand's Nightcap
> Book 3: The Gunslinger's Charlatan
> Book 4: The Deputy's Confidant

The Royal Engagement
> Prequel: Royal Ring
> Book 1: Royal by Design
> Book 2: Royal Coronation

Stand Alones
> Wedding Merger

Small Town Love, Sass, and Gossip
> Book 1: Bakery Wars
> Book 2: Playing It Queer
> Book 3: Booked For Love

Acknowledgement

To all the people I care for, I hope you enjoy this story. I know many of you don't read contemporary or romance novels. Trust me, I know that Hallmark isn't your channel of choice. That said, this was one way for me to write all of you into one place. Yes, maybe I should've added dragons. Many of you would've preferred it. But alas, this is where I landed.

Please enjoy!

I love you all!

Chapter 1 – Hope Retreat

The trees covering the hills up ahead looked dark and foreboding, but the sun behind them breathed fire in reds and oranges across the sky as it dipped low, saying its final goodnight.

Despite the distraction of the vivid sunset, I couldn't keep the smile from my face, or the excitement bubbling within, that had me dancing in my seat. I knew Nate would tell me to stop bouncing ... again, but I'd begged for this, and he'd finally said 'yes.'

"How much longer, do you think?" I clasped the seat ahead of me and gazed at the land whipping past the window of the bus.

With a sigh of contentment, I turned and smiled at the couple behind me. They both looked as happy as I did. *What were their names? Why was I so bad at remembering names?* They were a lesbian couple from ... Oshkosh? Oconomowoc? Oxford? One of those 'O' named cities. Locations were no easier for me to remember than names. I wish I were better; they'd been so nice to us since this program began.

"Not long," The pregnant woman said. "If I remember from the pamphlet correctly, we have two days to meditate, relax, and learn at the center, and then we take a ride to the hot springs."

My nose scrunched up as I tried to recall the brochure we'd all been given. As excited as I'd been for this trip, we'd read it right away, but that had been weeks ago.

The man across the aisle—Greg? Tony? Fuck my Swiss cheese brain!—leaned over. "It should be about fifteen more minutes. Two days at the center, a thirty-minute bus ride to the hot springs, and then we'll spend two days there in the cabins." He smirked. "It gives us all time to have the babies."

The pregnant woman behind me sighed. "And do they truly expect all of us to have our babies in this two day window? There are seven of us who are pregnant on this retreat."

I laughed. "Can you imagine? Are you honestly due?"

She made a sound halfway between a laugh and a whimper. "God, I wish." Her hands began to massage her large belly, similar to mine. "I'm tired of being kicked, especially in my bladder. My due date is in three days, but my doctor said it wouldn't be for another week, maybe two." Her voice changed. "First births are notoriously late. Don't expect your little one to show her face any time soon."

Groans from other pregnant women came from around us. From the back, one lady said, "Is that a script that they have to tell us all? Why give a forty week gestation if they genuinely mean forty-one or forty-two? Gah! I just want this kid out of me."

That turned everyone's dour sounds to laughter.

From the front of the bus, the driver mumbled, "Whoa, what the—" Then his voice got louder. "Everyone, brace yourselves!"

The back of the bus slid to the right, towards the ditch, and Nate's arm wrapped around me, tight. "Val!" His scream swirled around, lost in the sounds of everyone else's voices.

Oh, God! The bus doesn't have seatbelts. I wasn't sure what Nate hoped to accomplish by holding me, but I leaned into him anyway. His heat was always a comfort to me.

Then I felt, as well as saw, the driver try to turn the steering wheel the other way. A high pitched whine preceded the bus jerking to a sudden stop. *We crashed? Did we crash? Fuck? What's going to happen to us? Will our babies be okay?* My arms wrapped tightly around my stomach.

Will we survive?

Suddenly, my body floated up off the seat as I went weightless.

For a moment it felt glorious, then reality crashed back into me. *No, no, no, no, no! The life within me! This can't be happening.*

The bus ... an accident? No!

God! Help us all!

"I think this one's still alive."

"Thank God that one is. Maybe we can save more than just the babies."

Cool fingers touched my neck, my temple, my arm, and I shivered. "She is, but I don't know if we can keep her that way. I'm afraid, like the others, our only hope is to save the baby."

"Babies," I croaked out, my face wet with tears. I tried to lift an arm, but it was too heavy ... or maybe secured down. A shiver wracked my body, but I focused on only one thing. "Please, don't let them die." Numb ice filled my body, my soul. As much as my survival meant to me, as long as the babies lived, I knew I could pass on in peace.

"What?" The first person, an older woman, leaned down. "Did you say something, dear? Can you hear us?" Louder she yelled. "She's awake!"

"There are ta ... ta," I had to make them understand. With everything in me, I forced the word through numb, disobedient lips as a rapid, high-screeched whine rose in pitch and speed. Frantic, my heart pounded harder. They had to figure out my stumbling words. "Ta ... ta ... twins." The word came out in a sob that I tried to swallow. "Nate? Can I see Nate? Am I going to die? Will my babies die?" Tears streamed down my face.

The woman's voice relaxed me as I realized she'd deciphered at least some of my rambling. "Twins. There are two." She said, her voice ringing out to the others in the area. Then she spoke lower. "We will do everything we can to save your babies, ma'am." My body relaxed, trembling with relief, as the ceiling above me flashed past: tile, tile, tile, light. Tile, tile, tile, light.

Rosy

In awe, I gazed at the key in the center of the dining room table. *This is really real, after all this time ... it's mine.*

My hands trembled as I headed to the kitchen to make ramen noodles for dinner. I could afford to make something nicer—like mac and cheese—but the belt would be tight until ... I gulped.

From the living room, Dad laughed. "Stop gaping at the key and breathe."

"But look at it, Dad. The key is ... it's really real. Tomorrow we're opening up Road's Café and Bakery for the first time. It's ..."

"I know, sweetheart. This has been your dream. And tomorrow we'll wake up nice and early and meet customers for the first time."

I debated making coffee, but knew I needed to sleep. The grand opening of the bakery deserved me at my best.

A shiver of excitement wound its way down my spine at the thought, *my bakery*, and I managed to not giggle.

Just as I was about to turn off the light in the kitchen, my phone rang. Checking the display, I didn't recognize the number and debated ignoring it, but picked it up with a shrug. "Hello?"

"Ms. Roads?"

"Speaking." Years ago I read that you never said 'yes' in case phone trolls recorded the word and used it against you. The warning has always stuck with me causing me to always be careful with what I said.

"It's Divinity General Hospital. There has been a horrible accident." A boulder sized lump formed in my stomach, and I started to pace. Was it my best friend, Cindy? One of my neighbors? Who else would the hospital be calling about?

Three years ago I'd gotten a similar call about my mom and though my dad sat in the other room, my eyes immediately began to mist.

"How ... um," I took a breath. "How can I help you?" The steadiness of my voice surprised me.

The administrator went on to explain about a pregnancy retreat, seven pregnant women, a horrible accident, and no adult survivors. "We have ... well, several of the babies don't have any living family in the area to take them in. We're searching to see if they have anyone, at all, willing to care for them, maybe even adopt them. While we do our due diligence, you are on both the foster and the adoption list. We'd like to place one of the babies with you, temporarily, to foster. If we can't find any of the child's biological family, and everything works out with you and the baby, we may look into adoption in the future."

For a moment, I didn't know how to feel. All those families ... I couldn't even imagine. So much death. At the same time, my body trembled with the release of tension knowing that no one I knew had been in that accident. *They're all safe tonight. And a baby? I'm going to be a mom?*

My legs gave out and I sat hard on the solid wooden dining room chair. From the living room, Dad called out, sounded worried. "Rosy? Everything okay in there?"

Over the line, the man's words were insistent. "Ms. Roads, are you there? I'm afraid I need an answer."

Head spinning, I managed to breathe out. "Yes."

Chapter 2 – But What About Me?

Nora

Twelve Years Later ...

The sun streamed in the office, making the red woodgrain in my desk glow. I smiled, stroking the cool wood, loving the piece of furniture I practically spent a month's salary to purchase. I'd debated buying something so luxurious, especially since most of the thing was covered with papers, personnel files, recipes, and pictures my daughter had drawn, not to mention her track practice schedule. All that said, at the end of the day, I loved it.

"What do you think?" Fiona, my assistant, Fe for short, sounded excited, her voice light and chipper. "I know you think we should be heading in a new direction, and I think this would be a great location."

Right, work, expansion. This had been my idea after all.

"You think Pekara is big enough?"

"I do, it may not be the largest city, but it's great. It's a destination people go to."

I shook my head, looking at the state map. "I did say I wanted to head towards Madison, and it does split the difference between here and there."

"It does. You started off here in Milwaukee and now have two local bakeries. Your regulars love supporting us, as you know. To this day we can barely keep up. Then there are the two locations in Racine and Kenosha. I know everyone thinks your plan was to head towards Chicago, but I agree with you, we should stay in Wisconsin."

Despite the fact that Fe, who'd worked with me since I started branching out, was just repeating what I'd been saying, her excitement was almost too much. "What aren't you telling me, Fe?" Shaking my head, I lifted a hand, and squeezed my eyes shut. "I know this place. Why do I know this town? It's more than a tourist trap. More than a fly over, drive by, from here to the capital, what is it known for?" My eyes snapped open and I tapped my finger on a stack of folders. "Our initial studies ... there's an ice cream factory there." As I imagined the town, more pieces fell into place. "And ..." I grunted as I tried to think. "That town has a bakery already, doesn't it?"

Fe sighed. "It does."

"So, you think we should go in and compete with a local establishment? Is the current place bad? Unpopular? Going out of business? Why do you think competing with them is a good idea?"

Slumping in her seat, Fe's shoulders shrugged. "I don't know. The Road's Café and Bakery opened up about ten or twelve years ago. From what I can tell, the townspeople like it well enough."

"Then why?" A picture on a bookcase along the wall caught my attention. Gilly, my adopted daughter, ran across a field, holding a bunch of balloons of every color which trailed behind her. It was the kind of picture where a person could hear the peals of laughter as she ran. Shaking my head, I checked my watch and realized how late it was. Her au pair would be with her, but that wasn't enough. When I adopted her, I promised myself I would make her a priority. I'd been doing a good job these last twelve years, but I didn't want to fail now. The teen years were critical. "You know what? It doesn't matter. Find a place for us to stay there for the summer. I want to get a feel for this town before I decide to build."

A slow smile took over Fe's face. "Truly? What about running the office here?"

"You can do it. You practically do it anyway. You can call with any questions; it's only an hour away."

Back at home, I found Gilly and Delia, the au pair, in the living room yelling at the television. Gilly slammed her fists into the couch. "What are you doing? You can't add those ingredients together and expect the cookies to taste good. Are you slow?"

"Does this mean you're ready to start learning to bake?" Ever since she was young, Gilly had loved watching baking shows, but always refused to learn the craft. She knew a lot about baking theories, but was at a loss in the kitchen.

"Ma'ooom, no!" She leapt up to give me a hug. "Stop with that. I don't want to bake, you know that. All I want to do is run and jump and eventually go into medicine, like Delia ... or therapy ... or teaching ... or—"

"Yes, I know. You have lots of ideas, and none of them revolve around the kitchen." Laughing, I hung my purse by the door and went into the kitchen to start dinner, though by the smell of the house, someone had beaten me to it.

Delia followed me in. "I made a lasagna today. It should be done in twenty minutes."

"You're a doll. I can get some garlic bread and a salad made." I turned back towards the living room. "Gilly, can you come in here? We need to talk."

With a groan suited for the teen she wasn't yet, she trudged in and sat at the island. *God! We're only at twelve. What will I do when she's actually a teenager?*

"What's up?" She took a banana and started to peel it.

There was no way my next few words wouldn't start a fight with this child who was my world. I couldn't believe how much I loved her. "School gets out in a couple of days. After that, we're going to go on vacation."

Her eyes widened, then narrowed into a professional level glare. "A vacation or a work related 'on location' type thing I'm going to hate?"

"Probably more of the second." I admitted. "We're going to go to Pekara for—"

"No!" Gilly's eyes widened and she shook her head. "I have plans for the summer. My friends, my running, my piano, my—" her head whipped around the room looking for anything. "My life! I can't just up and leave, Mom. You can't make me."

A long deep sigh left me and I nodded. "Actually, I can. You're only twelve and without me here there won't be food or air conditioning. Who will take you to all those places? You can't stay here alone."

"I won't be alone. Delia will be with me. It's how it usually is anyway." Gilly's arm snapped out to indicate the au pair.

Both Delia's hands lifted. "I'm not getting into the middle of this. I go where all of you go. And since I'm from Pekara, I'd be more than happy to spend the summer there."

Maybe that's why I remembered the town. From when I hired Delia ... maybe? There was something else about it though. It's niggling at the back of my mind.

Having her support validated my decision. I was about to say more, when Gilly's icy blue eyes bore into me. "I'm going to an advanced high school in two years here in *Milwaukee*. If I spend my summer in some backwater, farm country, turned-around town, where all the people my age probably need their fingers and their toes to count, I'll probably lose a year or three of my education. Do you know what you're doing to my future by taking me there?" Her voice rose in teenage dramatic fashion as she built up steam.

I opened my mouth to respond, but Gilly shook her head. "No, I'm not done. I want to get on the track team early. There's a running program at the high school. I was hoping to join it. What will I do now?" She turned to Delia. "I'm right, aren't I? Tell me I'm right. Tell Mom!" She ended by slapping the counter as if she'd made some monumental proclamation, cementing her case.

One of Delia's eyebrows rose. "You did hear where I said that Pekara is my home town, right? Or were you already in your own world and ignoring the rest of us?"

Gilly's eyes widened and her jaw dropped open. She looked as if she wanted to say something before she slumped.

"There is an amazing day camp that will challenge you, and believe it or not, people run even in small towns." Leaning back on the counter, I crossed my arms. I didn't like that Gilly had been so rude and arrogant. "If I remember correctly, they have schools there that do teach you how to count beyond fingers and toes. That said, if you completely hate the camp and all of the other people your age, we can figure out what to do. The track program is in July and runs for six weeks. Pekara is just under an hour from here. We *could* just drive back and forth, you know. It isn't like we're days away."

The alarm went off, and Delia pulled the lasagna from the oven. Behind her, I slipped in the garlic bread to bake. By the time the main course was cool enough to serve, everything should be ready to eat.

"I just don't think there's anything in that small town that would interest me." Gilly crossed her arms and jutted out her chin.

Leaning on the counter, Delia smirked. "How about this, I know that at least one person from town has been to the Olympics."

I turned to keep Gilly from seeing my smile. Attending an event *could* mean as a spectator. Shooting a quick look, I did see her gape.

"No way! Really?"

Delia snorted. "You'll just have to come to town and find out, Miss Skeptical."

Glad the tension was lessened, I served plates to everyone. "So, ready for a new adventure?"

Chapter 3 – A Night On The Town

Rosy

"**M**om! Can I have the Snickerdoodle Pumpkin cookie? Oh, wait. I want the cookie that looks like a cup! It's filled with caramel. No wait, I want the Rainbow Sugar cookie with strawberry sauce."

Smiling down at her son Reggie, Tonya, a regular at the bakery, closed her eyes for a moment, then nodded. "Can you add to our order one each of what he asked for, and a Red Velvet stuffed cheesecake cookie for me? And a large coffee."

"Of course." Turning, I added the three individual cookies for the boy and the one for her to the larger order. Her company had a standing order for their monthly meetings. I gave her a total and she handed me a credit card.

"The problem, Rosy, is you're too good at making cookies. Don't get me wrong, the rest of your offerings are amazing, but these cookies." Her eyes scanned the display and she shook her head. "Have you ever thought about opening another branch?"

I laughed. "No, there's only me and Dad. We have plenty to do running one shop. We don't need the stress of worrying about doing more."

For a moment, Tonya stood, eyes squeezed shut. She opened them and smiled. "Once you've come to the smart decision, give me a call. We'll figure things out. In the meantime, think about hiring help. Don't you make enough by now? Once you've trained a few extra bakers, opening up your second and then your third shop will be a breeze, my friend."

Her words echoed those I'd heard from both Dad and my best friend, Cindy. I forced my face to stay blank so she wouldn't see my annoyance. Once I knew she couldn't read my expression, I forced a small smile. "I'll let you know if I change my mind."

After a nod, she took her sweets and headed out of the store, Reggie tight on her heel.

Before the door shut, Sacia blew in, her blond hair flying out behind her, blue eyes shining. "Mom, that's it! I'm done! It's summer!"

Behind her, smiles equally big, Charlie and Pris trotted in. The three of them had been inseparable since they were babies. "Hello, my troublesome Three Musketeers."

Charlie—Charlotte—and Pris—Priscilla—were twins. Despite that, they didn't look much alike. Charlie was a few inches shorter with straight dark hair, cut in a stylized bob that matched Sacia's, and green eyes. Pris had strawberry blond hair which she wore long and wavy, and brown eyes. All three girls were survivors of a bus crash that had killed their pregnant parents, forcing their early births. Because of this, and the fact that none of them looked alike, they called themselves the triplets.

The twins had been adopted by a neighbor. We'd realized it a couple months after the fact at a local park. Once the connection was found, our two families decided to bring the girls up with full disclosure. They'd been thick as thieves ever since.

They'd done everything together, from school, to breaks, to spending a ton of time in the bakery learning everything they could about the craft—from baking to eating anything they could get their hands on. In the last couple of years, they'd been more help than hindrance, all three of them able to give general help and each with different baking specialties.

Charlie scooted up to the display. "Mom said you couldn't get Sacia into the camp. Is that right? She may be able to bully someone, or maybe we all could do something else together." There was a note of desperation in her voice.

From the back, Dad grunted. "A few calls fixed it, don't worry. The terrible trio won't be separated. You'll all be out of our hair in a week. Thank all that is good in the world."

All three girls squealed and I heard Dad chuckle. He loved the three as if they were all his granddaughters, doting on them whenever he could.

Pris spun. "Okay, let's head home and start planning."

Before I could say another word, they were gone, along with their whirlwind twelve-year-old energy.

A few more customers came through the shop before I heard Cindy's gusty sigh as the door shut. "I can't believe you're still here."

Dad's heavy steps came up from the back, his apron covered in flour and chocolate. "Yes you can."

A smile broke out over Cindy's face and she winked at him. "True." Then her eyes narrowed at me, the dark brown pinning me down. "You promised me we'd have tonight to celebrate."

"But—"

"No," she snapped out. "It's your birthday. Mitch said he'd watch Sacia. Come on."

Dad squeezed my shoulders. "I did, sweetie. I can finish up here and close up. Sacia's with her friends, and we'll hang out tonight. I rented every scary movie I could find, and if she doesn't like that, I'm sure I can find some porn." His brows rose to emphasize his joke and he waved his hands in a shooing motion. "Now go, get dressed up nice and fancy. You remember how to do that, right?"

After scrunching my face up at him, I gazed down at my apron, stained with vanilla and cookie icing. I sighed. "Fine. I'll go. But not too late, I still have to wake up before the sun. The morning crowd are my best customers."

Dad gave me a shove. "I can open as well. I'm up at four anyway. Just take a few hours and try to remember how to be young. You do know you're more than a mom and businesswoman, right?"

Cindy laughed as I grumbled, but I hung up the apron and followed my friend out.

We sat at the Four Corners Bar, one of Pekara's nicer drinking holes ... well, it's the only one, if you didn't want to stick to every surface you dared to touch.

"I can't believe you convinced me to come here." I sipped the gin and tonic, relaxing back in the seat. "You know it isn't like I'll find anyone here. Not only do I know just about everyone around ... every woman is straight or unavailable, not to mention, as one of the only other lesbians, you are in a committed relationship. Honestly, what's the point? You mix better drinks, and it would've been cheaper at your place."

Cindy lightly punched my shoulder. "Would you relax and have some fun? You haven't had a night out in ages. It's like the moment you got the bakery and Sacia, you decided to give up on you. Yes, our town is small. Maybe I should've dragged you closer to Milwaukee, but it is what it is."

"Speaking of Ms. Right. How are you and Selena doing?"

"Good. It's just that, I moved into her place a couple of weeks ago, right?"

I held up my overpriced drink for her to clink in cheer. "And it's as wonderful as you'd always hoped, even though you now live on the other side of town and I don't get to see you as much." Gazing at her, I pouted as dramatically as I could, leaning in and giving her my biggest puppy dog eyes.

"It's not you I miss, it's the girls." She snorted. "They are way more fun than you, Ms. Works All The Time."

Slumping, I couldn't even argue her point. "Fine, so, what do you want to tell me about cohabitation?"

"She has a cat."

"You love cats. That's a good thing."

Putting down her drink, Cindy rubbed her face. "I do love cats, and this cat is amazing. But the thing is, when we first moved in, I'm not sure if Selena told me the cat's name or not, and now it's been long enough ... would it be weird for me to ask?"

A laugh bubbled up from my center. "You don't know its name? What does the old ball and chain call it?"

"Well, that's just it. She calls the cat something different every time she's around it. 'Snuggle-Puss', 'Fluffy-Butt', 'Idiot', you know, cat nick-names."

"So what do you do?"

"The same for now, but I figure eventually I'll have to learn the Fluff-Balls name."

We both laughed. I couldn't believe she'd gotten herself into this predicament. No, I could, it was so her style.

I took another sip, admitting the drink went down well. A yawn threatened to take me under, and I narrowed my eyes at my friend. "How long do I have to pretend I'm awake?"

"Until you admit you're having fun."

Tony, the bartender, came over with a platter of cheese curds. "Complements of the house, birthday girl." He winked before walking off. We both watched him return to the bar.

"Fine, I'll stop complaining. Tonight *has* been fun." Looking over the faces of the people in the room, I recognized customers that would come in early for coffee and a treat. Some went for cookies, others for cupcakes. The bakery didn't have a huge selection beyond those two specialty items, but what we did create was popular.

A jolt to my shoulder and Cindy's laugh brought me back to our conversation. Cindy pointed with her chin. "Do you know her?" At the bar sat a woman with short brown hair, shaved on the sides, but longer on top. The tips were highlighted. She wore a dark business suit. In the low lighting it was hard to tell if it was blue or gray.

"I haven't seen her at the bakery. She must be driving through. Got lost on her way to Milwaukee or Madison ... or maybe Chicago. She doesn't genuinely feel like a Pekara kind of gal."

"Go talk to her," Cindy urged, pushing my shoulder.

"What? No. She doesn't seem like she wants to be disturbed."

Cindy rolled her eyes. "She's at a bar. Just ... go. If she wants to be alone, ask Tony for another round."

Grumbling, I clenched my jaw tight as I stood, smoothed out my dress, wishing my stomach were flatter, and headed to the empty seat next to Ms. Power Suit.

Behind the bar, Tony quirked a smile. "Another gin and tonic, Rosy? Or are you here to tell me how fantastic the cheese curds are?"

After I forced my jaw to relax, I smiled. "Yeah, Tony, another drink would be great."

"I'll put it on Cindy's tab. Your bestie should be good for it on your birthday."

I closed my eyes and breathed slowly. *Why did he have to say that so loudly? Was everyone in this town out to get me?*

"It's your birthday?" The woman next to me asked, her voice low and sultry. It sent chills down to my toes.

Releasing my breath, I opened my eyes, and smiled at her. She was even more beautiful up close. Her makeup perfectly accented her cheek bones and luscious lips, which lifted on one side in amusement. And her light green eyes sparkled.

Tony placed the drink in front of me and I took a sip, trying not to tremble. "Yeah, birthday." I shook my head. I wasn't a teen anymore, I could do this. "Yes, I'm thirty-seven today." With a smile I lifted my glass in cheer.

She tapped her glass with mine. "Well, happy birthday, Rosy." My eyes widened, then I remembered Tony saying my name when I approached. She continued, "I'm Nora."

"Nice to meet you, Nora."

We both sipped our drinks, and my birthday got a lot better.

Chapter 4 – Your Place Or Mine?

Nora

"Nice to meet you, Nora." The brunette sat on the barstool next to me. She was curvaceous in all the right ways. I was tired of women who tried to be model thin all the time; this Rosy looked like someone I could ... *stop it, Elenora Shifer, you are here on business, not to flirt with some random local!*

The bartender put a drink in front of Rosy and he winked at her. She blushed. *Great, she's probably into men.*

The woman's gaze shifted back to me and her blush intensified. *God, she's sexy. I wonder how low that blush goes. Does it color her ...*

With a deep breath, I closed my eyes. Drink or no drink, I had to get my mind under control. Fe had set up a few places for me to tour so I could find a place for us to stay this summer. This was a quick in and out trip. Not the best time for a one-night stand. Hell, my appointment was tomorrow at eight. The only reason I ventured out of the hotel room was the volume of the people in the next room over. I had to wonder, letting myself drink in the sultry woman next to me, if I'd been more annoyed or jealous with that other couple. It'd be a long time since I'd been with anyone else.

Rosy's face fell and I realized the silence between us had grown too long. As her body tensed to get up, I made a snap decision, it wasn't like talking with her would hurt anything. "So, thirty-seven?"

Her face lit up the room when she smiled and a sparkle came to her eyes ... a stormy gray blue. "Yeah, I know. I guess I'm not supposed to admit my age, right? Maybe I should've said twenty-five," she snorted, then slapped her hands over her mouth for a moment, "not that I could hope to pull that off. But it's a sexier age, no?"

A small groan escaped her and she quickly picked up her drink and took a sip. Her babbling was adorable. People were often nervous around me in meetings, but this was something new. It had nothing to do with my running a chain of successful bakeries.

When Rosy finally lifted her gaze back to me, I lifted an eyebrow, then smiled. "I don't know, at thirty-seven you're still a baby. If you dropped your age by twelve years I may be arrested if I were caught speaking with you."

Her mouth dropped open, then she slowly let her eyes travel down and up my body, taking it all in. I knew how I looked and smirked as she made it back to my face. "You're older than me? There's no way." Her tongue darted out to lick her bottom lip, then she bit it.

I want to bite that lip. With a force of will, I didn't follow through with the thought ... barely. "I'm forty-one."

Her brows shot up. "That's barely older than me. We're practically the same age."

"I'm in a whole different decade."

She laughed and finally relaxed, and her beauty shone through. *What is wrong with me? I'm only here for a couple of days. Calm down, Nora!*

After taking another sip, she asked, "So, what are you doing in Pekara? Got lost on your way to somewhere more exciting?"

It was my turn to laugh. "No, this is actually exactly where I wanted to be. Your friend hired me to entertain you." Eyes wide, I kept my face blank.

Rosy's jaw dropped. Her head jerked back and forth, looking between me and the friend she came with and it appeared she was ready to bolt.

Right before she stormed off, I placed a hand on her arm, momentarily distracted by the silky smoothness of her skin and the electricity of the connection, I shook my head, then smiled. "I'm kidding. I don't even know who your friend is. I'm here for a day, then I'm heading back home tomorrow." Not wanting to break our connection, I rubbed my hand on her arm. "Did you know you're fun to play with?" My voice dropped for the last part. I thought she'd be fun for many other types of games.

Her eyes narrowed. "Here for the day? What could you possibly want to do? Case out the joint?

Are you a thief? Or are you thinking of moving here?"

"Those are the only two options you can think of? Robbery or relocation?"

"Or you're lost, yes, pretty much." Rosy's head bobbed up and down as she agreed with the three reasons for being in town.

"Doesn't Pekara have a big tourist draw?" *The only reason I chose this town was because that was my understanding. Enough traffic to make opening a bakery here worth it. Especially since there's already one in town I'd have to compete with.*

I didn't want to think about that other bakery. Though I'd kept my face out of the public eye, there was a chance that the owners of Road's Cafe and Bakery would recognize me from somewhere. It had been impossible to never be in the news. If I wanted to check the place out, I'd have to send in Fe or trust their online images.

"Oh, I guess it does. Most people come for a day or two. We have a few things that bring people in. You just look classier than that." Rosy interrupted my thoughts.

"You don't think I've come to tour a cheese factory? Visit the chocolate factory? Or see how the best ice cream in the state goes from concept to cone?"

"Oh, that last one is pretty great." Rosy winked. "As long as you're not interested in an actual ice cream shop, the factory isn't great at its end game."

"Maybe I'll give it a go, though I don't know if I'll have time." *At least not this time. I bet Gilly would love it. It's possible she'll get over her stink if I tell her about all the town's sugars. Maybe she'd be less prickly about spending the summer here.*

Shaking my head, I realized I had to focus. *I need to change the subject before I ask Rosy out or do something else stupid.* "So, what are your birthday plans?"

She held her hands out to the side to encompass the bar and the two of us, then shrugged.

Again, one of my eyebrows scooted up my face. "This can't be it. I mean, it's a Thursday night, what about the rest of the week, the weekend, hell the rest of the month? Don't you have big plans? You're thirty-seven, aren't you going to live it up large?"

A decisive snort and eye roll was a pretty solid answer. Then Rosy turned slightly away, as if the question offended her, and sipped her drink.

A sense of dread filled me. I didn't want my time with the alluring woman to end ... not yet. "What did I say?"

She sighed. "Nothing. I just ..." Her hands scrubbed at her face before they fell to her sides. "I don't usually go out; too many responsibilities. I know ... something else I shouldn't talk about when meeting a gorgeous woman for the first time, but I don't remember the last time I spoke to someone new ... or beautiful, or well—" she ducked her head. "I don't get out much."

Heat exploded in me at her words. Images of Rosy, naked, on my bed flashed through my mind. Licking her from head to toe. I tried not to react to all the thoughts, but if she had half the curves that outfit promised ...

I couldn't stop the groan.

"Maybe, if you were planning on being out late with your friend, you could give yourself a birthday gift." *Am I honestly suggesting this?*

She breathed in sharply. "What are you thinking? That ice cream tour? Because I've been on it—"

Leaning over, I stopped her words with a kiss. I meant it to be light and flirty, but once our lips met, she gasped, and I couldn't resist. Our tongues met, and God, her taste. A searing heat filled my veins and I wrapped a hand into her hair. One of hers landed gently on my hip, and began to stroke in slow circles.

The sounds of the bar, loud talking, louder music, clinking glasses, and all the rest faded away, until all that remained was the heat between me and Rosy.

Her hand slowly rubbed up to my waist and mine dipped lower, over her shoulder, down to her—

Someone cleared their throat too close to us to be ignored. We jerked apart turning in towards the bar.

Rosy's head dropped into her hands. "Hi Tony."

"Not that I don't love the show—probably most of the bar does—but it does make sales a bit harder."

After giving us each one last glare ... an amused glare, he sauntered off.

Looking over to the other woman, I realized she was laughing. I chuckled too. "Would you want to join me back at my hotel? If you couldn't spend the night, I get it, but maybe for a few hours?" Now that I had her taste, I wanted more. She was like a cream puff, which I loved, and I'd only gotten a nibble.

Her eyes did that back and forth between me and her friend again, and then a wide smile split her face. "Yeah, sure, I'd really like that."

I dug in my wallet and tossed some bills on the bar for a tip, then clasped her hand in mine. We slid through the crowd to the exit, only a few people called out cheers to Rosy. When I checked, to my amusement, she'd blushed an even darker red. *Who knew it was possible?*

The hotel and bar were only a couple of blocks apart, so I'd walked. We'd made it a block, when my phone buzzed. "Can you give me a second? I need to see who this is."

She shrugged.

'Mom. Tammy and Donna said that if I'm not in Milwaukee this summer they'll no longer be my friends. I hate you. I hate you forever!'

Cold dread wiped away any heat and desire from the last hour. I wanted to scream. The over dramatics of kids.

Blowing out a breath, I turned to Rosy. "I am so sorry, I can't ignore this ... it's important. Can we take a rain check?"

The look on her face told the whole story. Apparently, this kind of disappointment was not only expected, it was an old friend.

She bowed her head. "Sure, whatever. Until the next time you happen to be in Pekara and I'm out and about."

Before I could ask, or get her number, or anything, she spun, and headed down the street. Between Gilly and this, I suddenly felt like I'd gone into a boxing ring and thoroughly lost.

Chapter 5 – A Day In The Life Of Gossip Central

Rosy

The kitchen was a hotbed of activity. Since arriving this morning, I'd made several batches of cookies and Dad had been busy with cupcakes.

As customers came in, we switched who ran out to greet them, though usually it was me. Dad tended to be more gruff.

During the times he took the counter, I let my mind wander to Nora and the night that could've been. I wasn't sure if I was happy or sad our evening had been cut short. It had been years since I'd been with anyone. *What was I thinking, leaving the bar with her?* Then again ... gah, she was so gorgeous, way out of my league.

At just after seven, I was cracking eggs when the bell rang.

"On it." Dad patted himself down and lumbered to the front.

"Mitch! You're not usually the one to come out here. Rosy's letting you out of the dungeon?" Lucas Weber, Charlie and Pris's dad, laughed and I heard the girls scuttling around the counter a moment before they descended on the kitchen.

"Well, you know how it is." Dad laughed. "So tell me, are you here just to drop off the girls, or do you want anything?"

"Mom! You're making cookies without me? You'll ruin them." Sacia came over and started helping me to form the next tray.

From across the kitchen, the twins stood, both looking deceptively sheepish. The two didn't have a pensive bone in either of their bodies. "Out with it!"

Before they could answer, I could hear the cash register ding, and my dad chuckle. "Well, you know what they say, 'If I look this much like a cupcake, I must make a great tasting one' ... or dozen!" *It was his favorite saying.* Both men laughed. "Enjoy the selection. We'll keep the girls tonight and drop them off tomorrow."

Lucas grunted. "Perfect. We're taking them to Six Flags tomorrow. I'm hoping it won't be too busy. Camp can't start soon enough. This much energy times three ... why can't we bottle and sell it? We'd be rich!"

"We would."

I focused on the girls, who'd all been listening to the plans for their adventures. They knew, but hearing about the amusement park had all of them distracted and glowing.

"Charlie, Pris, what's up?"

Pris straightened her shoulders and tried to stand taller. "Can we try to make padded shoes?"

Next to her, Charlie's eyes widened looking hopeful.

I took a moment to tamp my laugh down into a small smile. "And if you make pâte à choux, what will you do with the dough?"

Taking a small step forward, as if she felt her victory were near, Pris said, "I want—" Charlie reached out to slap her arm. "We want to make eclairs or puff balls. Charlie can make the cream for inside and I can decorate."

Dad had come in and narrowed his eyes at everyone. "You know, this is a bakery, not a negotiation situation. The current cupcakes come out in three minutes. I'll pull them, put the next batch in, and while the ones I pulled out cool, we'll make your fancy dough. Rosy and Sacia need to make cookies or we'll run out before noon."

The three girls squealed and Dad and I flinched.

As Dad and the twins made their first attempt at pâte à choux, Sacia kept sneaking glances. She had been decorating the cookies, then suddenly yelped.

"What's wrong, sweetheart?"

She waved her right hand vigorously, as if she were trying to fling it away. "Ow, ow, ow, ow, ow! I pinched my thumb."

My face scrunched up. "How do you pinch your thumb decorating cookies?"

"Mom! I'm hurt. Can we save the interrogation for later?" She looked at me like I'd grown a second head. *Is this what my future holds for me? Is this what life with teens will be like?*

"You can just use your left hand to do the majority of the work, you know."

"That's not how it works. Left hands are useless ... or at least mine is." She rolled her eyes. "Give me a few seconds, I'll be fine."

The next time the bell rang, I went to cover the counter. One of my regular customers, Melody, came in. She was part of a polycule. She, or one of her group, often came in on Saturdays to pick up a box of goodies.

"Morning Melody. How is everyone?"

Her smile warmed the room. I wasn't sure I knew anyone more positive than her. "Oh, you know. Things are great! Though, the weirdest thing happened."

I raised an eyebrow. I thought most things in her life were weird. During the day, she was a nanny, which you'd never guess if she didn't tell you. She seemed so ... sane. "Do tell."

"Well, you know my group, my polycule?" She waggled her brows.

"I do. Speaking of, your regular order or do you want to shake things up?"

Melody gazed at the display. "Add a few more of the cupcakes and some of the Sacia specials. Hers are always a bit better." She smiled widely. From the back, Sacia and the twins cheered and Dad groaned.

"Got it. Now what news do you have of your polycule?"

"Well, this new person, Callen, he showed up. No one's sure who he thinks he's there to connect with and date. He's just ... you know, there."

One of my brows lifted. "And are you letting him stay?"

"For now, sure." Melody shrugged. "We have the space and he's taken to cooking and cleaning the kitchen, as if that's his domain. The thing is, he's a good cook, so we're all trying to be chill. It's only been a few days, so I'll keep you informed, as always. It's just that I'm worried we may have to kick him to the curb if we can't figure this situation out, soon."

After ringing up the price and handing Melody the box, she paid and left. At the door she turned. "You know, *you* could always join us. You're sexy and the others have agreed you'd be a great addition."

Blushing to my toes, I waved as her laughter matched the twinkling of the bell. *This is the second time in as many days someone has called me sexy. If I don't watch out, it could go to my head! God, I wish I'd gotten her phone number, if she were in town for more than one day, maybe we could actually go on a date.*

Before I could turn and face the firing squad, who clearly heard the full conversation, Cindy sauntered in. "Why are you the color of the cherries on your apron?"

With a sigh, I rubbed my face and shook my head. "Long story. We can discuss it later." I dropped my hands and saw the wide smile on her face.

"Perfect, we can discuss your birthday date then as well. Let's make it official, say, dinner tonight?"

Dad's voice came from the back. "Assuming you take these gremlins from my kitchen, I'll make sure you have your dinner with my daughter!"

"That's a deal, Mitch!" Cindy winked, then waggled her eyebrows. "Girls, let's go shopping. Do you have everything you need for camp?"

The cacophony of noise hurt my ears, but the sounds were all happy ones.

The three ran out, each wrapping me in a hug before they left. They weren't sticky, so Dad obviously made them wash. Then they, with Cindy, were out the door and the silence was almost as deafening.

Back in the kitchen, the room was a disaster. With a sigh, I rotated the latest batch of cookies in the oven, then started to clean.

Within the muck, I found the eclairs the twins had made. "How much did you help with these?" I took a bite and savored their creation.

"Not much. We found the recipe, but they did most of the work. All three girls are great bakers." Dad's smirk was all pride.

"We may have to let them play around with this. If they refine it, we could sell these. Give them the profits. I know their parents have been worried about starting a savings fund for them. This could be a start."

Dad nodded, smiling back. "I like it, Rosy. It's a good plan."

Chapter 6 – Competition Is All Around

Nora

The coffee was hot, almost too hot to drink, but it smelled good and soothed my soul. After missing out on an evening with Rosy ... God, that would've been a fun time ... but, the opportunity is gone, and I'm back in the real world. C'est la vida.

There was something about a quiet morning, away from the noise and hustle and bustle of—

"MA'OOOM! We have to leave soon, is breakfast ready?" Gilly's voice filled the house, replacing the warm calm, like a hug from your best friend, with the tension of mid-day traffic.

"Yes, love. I have oatmeal made. We can add fruit and nuts. There's orange juice or milk in the fridge."

"Yes to all of it." She ran through the kitchen half dressed, disappearing around the corner. "Where are my shorts?"

From the living room, Delia said quietly, "In the drier, like I told you last night."

"Oh, yeah, right."

Gilly ran back, the other way. "Be back in a sec."

I placed everything she requested by her seat. "Delia, what would you like?"

"I'll take the same. No, coffee instead of the other drinks." She stood and made her way to the kitchen island.

By the time I had three dishes served, Gilly had made it back and was digging in. "I'm so excited for this meet. It's the last of the season, and I'm going to kick butt. I'm going to beat those stupid—"

"Language."

"What? They are. The idea that they don't want to be my friends because I'm going away for the summer is dumb. You can't convince me otherwise." Her face tightened as she glared at me.

In all honesty, I couldn't disagree, but I didn't want to promote name calling. "They are being catty, I'll agree to that."

"Fine, I'll beat those catty ... um, girls." I had a feeling 'girls' wasn't the word she wanted to use, but she wasn't going to push it with me.

Before Gilly joined track, she didn't have any love of running. She'd joined because of friends. It didn't take long to realize that not only did she love the sport, she excelled at it. Well, now that those 'friends' had decided to drop her, I guess beating them was her new goal in life.

Delia leaned back. "So, which events are you competing in? One-hundred, two-hundred, and four by one-hundred. Those are a given. Anything else?"

For the last year, Gilly had been training in several. Her coach had been testing her out to see where she did the best.

Bouncing in her seat, Gilly said, "Coach put me down as an alternate for the four-hundred as well. That one would be challenging, but fun." She took a bite of her hot cereal, dancing in place. "Oh! And the long jump."

My mind whirled at the number of events the two listed off. "So, you're ready for all that?"

"Ma'ooom!" She wailed. Then she shook her head. "Whatever, you just don't understand."

Once everyone was done, and the plates cleared away, Gilly snapped her head to me. "What about treats? Did you buy anything?"

I froze in my tracks. "Wait, what? We're on snack duty for this last meet?"

"It's on the schedule." She gave me her teen look, which I still believed she was too young to have.

With slow movements, to not startle the teen, I rubbed my forehead. "Okay, I'll call Fe—"

"Ma'ooom!" *Gods, how many years would I be living with this wail?* "Not the bakery ... again! You're so predictable."

"Gilly!" I said her name with a teasing shake of my head. "I was thinking of having Fe pick the stuff up from a different bakery." *One that's an hour away, but the meet is twenty minutes in that direction ... so, not that horrible.*

Gilly shrugged. "Fine, whatever. As long as the treats are there by the end. And maybe not just sweets. Some of the girls like other options."

One of my brows popped up. "Honestly?"

She laughed. "Nope, gotcha!" And she ran towards the car.

"Go! Yes! Yes! You can do it!" I turned to Delia. "Did you see that? She smoked the other girls. Goodness, she's fast!"

"These meets are amazing. Not only are all the kids focused, but the crowds are electric. It's amazing." She agreed.

When they finally announced the girls one-hundred meter run, my insides clenched with nerves, but then the alarm sounded, and Gilly dashed off, her blond hair streaming behind her.

The other runners didn't have a chance.

It happened again during the two hundred meter run twenty minutes later.

"Hey boss, did I miss anything on my trip to Pekara? For part of the drive I was stuck behind a tourist bus and I didn't think I'd make it back for any of the meet." Fe sat down, two pink boxes in her arms. We'd saved two seats for her and the treats.

For a moment my mind whirled. Bus! *How could I forget? Pekara was where the bus had crashed, giving me the best gift of my life! How could anything ever top that?*

"Hello? Nora?"

I shook myself. "Sorry, distracted by my thoughts. You missed two of Gilly's runs. She's amazing, and I'm not just saying this because I'm her mother. Ask Delia; she's much less biased."

They both laughed. When another of Gilly's events was announced, we watched as she waited for the baton as the anchor runner. The other schools had some fast runners, and she wasn't the first to get the baton, but she was the first to cross the finish line.

The stands near them all erupted in cheers.

During the long jump, Gilly came in fourth, just off the podium. The girl could run, but she did have her limitations.

After all the events were over, the team met, and we placed the two boxes of bakery treats on the tailgate of a truck. Another parent had brought drinks, beef sticks, and string cheese.

"Nora, those don't look like your normal baked goods. Do you have new recipes you're testing out on us?" One of the parents laughed as he selected a cookie. He moaned in delight as he took a bite.

"No," I smiled. "This is from a different bakery, one from out of town. I decided to check out the competition and support someone else."

Everyone made shocked sounds, but the sweets started to disappear.

Bracing myself, I finally took one of the Red Velvet cookies. Wanting the thing to be horrible, I took a bite.

To my utter horror, it was one of the best cookies I'd ever tasted.

Chapter 7 – Rumor and Hearsay

Rosy

The ovens seemed to purr in the background. They didn't truly make any noise, not really, but I liked to think they enjoyed eating the different sweet treats, cooking them to the perfect doneness, then releasing them to the world, utterly and mouthwateringly scrumptious.

While I toiled away at the various cookies, Dad made cupcakes. He enjoyed creating the variety of pillowy creations as much as I loved the different cookies we sold. There were a few core cookies we had every day. Then I always had one or two creative ones. Some were on rotation as our regulars loved them. Breakfast waffle with bacon. Tiramisu, raspberry and ricotta, no matter what combination I whipped up, everyone seemed to enjoy them.

About once every month or two, Sacia came to me with an idea she wanted to try. A couple of weeks ago she asked if she could make Italian Rainbow cookies for pride month. It took a few attempts to make the special treats, but the end product looked and tasted amazing. There was a small section in the display cabinet devoted to her creations.

Now, we were going to devote a section to the twins. I hadn't spoken to their parents yet, but I didn't think they'd mind.

Mixing a batch of Red Velvet cookies, I imagined Nora wearing red velvet. Gah, I had to stop with her. I'd never again see the first woman in ages to take an interest in me.

So caught up in the dream of our next date—Thai food and dancing—I didn't hear when Dad's alarm went off, or when he approached the table where I worked. "Have you seen the latest news from Milwaukee?"

My heart skipped a beat and I nearly hit the ceiling in fright at the suddenness of his words. "Holy moly, Dad, I didn't hear you!"

"Obviously. I think the spoonful of dough you'd been scooping ended up in the light fixture."

My head fell back and I squinted. A small blob of red goo was on the light, mocking me. I grumbled as I went to the closet to get the ladder. The last thing I needed was for that to fall back into my bowl or to contaminate the rest of the cookies.

Once the offending bit of raw cookie was taken care of, and I'd put the ladder away, I got back to work. "Was there a reason for startling me, or were you having some sort of perverse fun?"

Dad chuckled. "Can it be both?" He waggled his brows at my glare. "As I asked, have you heard the latest from Milwaukee?"

"No, I try not to pay attention to anything that doesn't concern me. Why would I care?" With the tray finished, I swapped it with the one in the fridge, then put the one from the fridge into the oven, taking the baked cookies out to cool.

"Elinore Shifer, owner of Pie In The Sky and Heavenly Delights Bakery, is looking to open her fifth location. Sources close to the CEO say—"

I grunted. "What, that she's planning on heading to Chicago to take over there? She started in Milwaukee and has been slowly moving south realizing that Wisconsin isn't nearly a big enough challenge for her." Annoyance built in me and my motions began to get choppy. As if shocked, I stepped back and shook out my hands. I had to make sure my dough balls stayed consistent. "Why do you even bother with those magazines and gossip junk?"

"Rosy, our bakery is doing good, great even. It behooves us to understand the larger picture. Pie In The Sky *is* the larger picture here in Wisconsin." Dad spoke slowly, as if frustrated at having to explain the obvious to me.

"Have you ever tried their stuff? When Cindy and I were in Milwaukee, we stopped in one of the bakeries. They had a few cookies, chocolate chip, snickerdoodle, you know, the basics, and cupcakes. Behind the counter they had images of wedding cakes they'd made—"

With a sigh, Dad shook his head. "Speaking of cake, we need to start on the cake for this evening. I know they didn't want anything too fancy, but that needs to start soon."

I glared, knowing he was trying to change the subject. "I know. This is my last batch of cookies, and then I'll start on that order. Anyway, back to what I was saying. They had about five or six other types of things. Their bakery is much more diversified than ours. Fudge, brownies, blondies, tarts, it was ... I don't know, nothing we can—"

"Stop." Dad's voice whipped out. "They're in Milwaukee, we're in a town that loves us. And no one said anything about competing. The fact that we specialize isn't a bad thing. There are so many desserts in the world, a dozen bakeries could serve different things. As for brownies, blondies, and tarts, those are easy. We can add them if you want."

"Not really. Well, maybe brownies. My guess is, if we sold individual and full pans on shelves around the storefront, they'd go like hotcakes."

"I agree. And the girls would definitely help."

Excited about a new plan, I finished up the cookies and started on the cake for the wedding later that day.

The bell dinged and I tensed, ready to move to help the customer. When the sound of three loud and obnoxious girls reached me, I relaxed back into mixing ingredients.

"Mom! Oh my god, today is it, and then camp. Did you know they have swimming and a competition with all the sports, and horseback riding, and—"

I held up my hands. "Yes, I knew all of this. It's a camp, and I hope you have all the fun this summer."

Charlie came over. "It's so exciting!. We know the summer will be full of so much fun."

"But, we're worried about today and don't want to waste any of this summer." Pris's eyes widened.

"It's true! This is very important to us." Charlie sounded so sincere.

"Is there any chance of us going to a water park" Sacia's eyes widened and her lower lip quivered. "We just truly want to make the most out of this summer."

Wow they were laying it on thick. Much more of this and I'd need a trowel just to cross the room.

The large mixer was full of creamed butter and I started adding sugar. All three girls threw their most pitiful gazes at me, Charlie winning the prize, her lower lip quivering. With the practice of years, I stared at each of them in turn. "Gramps and I need to make this cake. You three need to be ready for tomorrow, and we have all summer to plan a trip to Illinois. You knew it wasn't going to happen today. Sunday is a busy day around here. Now, are you three going to help out or do you want to head back to the house?"

Sacia's face scrunched up as she thought.

Wiggling, Pris closed one eye and then opened it again, opting to close the other one, as if she thought better with one eye closed. "Can Charlie and I make eclairs again?"

"Yes," Dad answered right away. "And we're thinking of adding brownies to the bakery. I thought that while the cake is mixing and baking, Sacia could help me figure out some recipe ideas."

Suddenly all three girls leapt into action. Thankful that Dad could manage the girls, I focused on everything else.

The store's bell chimed again, and since the girls were already here, I made my way to the counter.

Cindy sauntered up to the counter and folded her arms on top of it, leaning forward to smile at me. "Hi birthday girl, you have a story to tell me." Her smile would put the Cheshire Cat to shame.

"No, I genuinely don't." I shook my head before reaching down to grab her one of the Italian Rainbow cookies. She always loved to try Sacia's special creations.

After trying the cookie, her face morphed into one of pleasure. "God that girl can bake!"

"Thanks, Cindy!" Sacia yelled from the back, her joy obvious.

"Of course, kiddo. You'll soon be a better baker than your mom."

"Soon?" The attitude in that one word sent shivers of pre-teen dred down my spine.

Cindy chuckled and spoke low. "You'll have fun with that one."

I heard Dad laughing as well before he said, "Let the cake layers cool for a few more minutes."

Head swinging around, Cindy gave a curt nod. "Good, we're alone. I have some good gossip."

"Well, you know that's the real reason I opened this bakery. It had nothing to do with baking or my love of creating new cookies. I just wanted a place to gather all the juicy news from town."

"Well duh!" Cindy waggled her brows. "So, there's a new guy at work, his name is Callen, he just moved here from Kenosha. From what I can tell, he'll be a great addition to the library, but you know we don't make much money."

"Yes, yes, I know, but remember, I'm working, hurry this along." Her story was broken up by the stream of customers who came in to buy their weekend sugar and coffee fixes.

"Okay, so Callen got here a week or so ago, and hadn't found a place to live. He was just going to hole up at the hotel, though it's way too expensive. He was at the bar, and found a guy he seemed to get along with. The guy invited him home to crash on his couch."

"So is Callen gay? Was there chemistry? Is our little town becoming more diverse?" This was beginning to become more interesting.

"Rosy, stop rushing me."

I scoffed. "Of course, why would I do anything of the sort, it isn't like I need to get back to baking, or anything."

Cindy chuckled and waved a hand. "Whatever, you have the whole crew back there. I know you have a cake to make, but since the layers have been made, Charlie and Pris can get them stacked and coated. And Pris is great at decoration. You're just needed for the final details."

The girls cheered from the back, and Charlie yelled, "You tell her, Cindy. We have the kitchen covered."

A low groan escaped me and I glared at my friend. "Just finish your story."

"Okay, so, I don't think he's gay, he just ... I don't know, more demi than anything else. He just needed a place to crash." Cindy's eyes widened and she leaned forward. "He's still there. I guess the guy lives in a flat with a few women, and they're all into free love. He just slinks into the kitchen, cooks a big meal, and once everyone has eaten, cleans up. Every now and then he'll put a list of groceries he needs on the fridge and a day or two later, it all appears bought and put away. No one has mentioned rent or any other pay. He doesn't know what to do, but it's just such a good situation, he's hoping they continue to overlook him."

Amusement bubbled up in me. "He's living with Melody, Franco, and Latina." I realized Callen was the name Melody had mentioned the other day.

"Yeah, he seems to have fallen in with our local polycule and has become their live-in chef. He's okay with the arrangement but doesn't want to ask them if they're okay with it in case they're not and kick him out." Though Cindy spoke to me, her focus was on the treats in the display.

I snorted. "Okay, that was a great bit of tea. How about your cat issue? Have you figured out the name yet?"

Cindy slumped. "No, not yet. Now, give me a box of goodies that I can take back home."

After she paid for the selection of sweets, I headed back to the kitchen to check on progress. The cakes were cooling and the twins had a tray of eclairs. They looked good enough to sell.

Before I could decide what to do with them, the bell rang, and I spun back to help the customer. The twin's mother walked in, smiling wide.

"Hi Sammi, how are you this fine Sunday?"

"I'm great. How about you?"

An idea struck. "Give me a moment." I slipped into the back, selected the nicest eclair, and brought it out to Sammi. "What do you think of this?"

She looked it over with a critical eye. This wasn't the first new item she'd inspected. Being in marketing, she was very picky. "It's an eclair. I love eclairs, by the way. This one looks professional, which I'd expect from you." She took a bite and her eyes widened. "Oh! It tastes great. Love! Five stars, would eat again."

Laughter and the sound of what I assumed were high fives erupted from the back. Sammi's eyes narrowed as she looked over my shoulder. I pointed with my chin. "I actually had nothing to do with this. Your daughters made it."

One brow shot up. "They did?"

"I was thinking of adding them above Sacia's Specialties. All proceeds could go to them, you know, into a college fund."

Sammi's eyes widened and her jaw dropped. "You don't have to do that. You've already done so much for the girls."

My hands shot up in a double stop sign. "Sammi, I'm not making these, they are. It's the least I can do. And it was their idea, their creativity. It should be their profits."

Sammi came around the counter to give me a big hug. "God, I don't know what brought you into my life, but thank you."

From behind, the girls joined in, engulfing me in a Weber family sandwich hug. Then the twins headed back to finish up in the kitchen.

Sammi pulled away and rubbed her eyes. "Okay, why don't I take the girls to a movie and Sacia can spend the night. I'll take them to camp tomorrow morning so you can get up at stupid-o-clock to have this place open."

I smiled. "Sounds great, thanks. I'll let Cindy know that she has tomorrow morning off."

A herd of elephants ... or the three girls, ran from the kitchen to follow Sammi out.

When I returned to the kitchen, it looked like a tornado had hit. A twelve-year-old tornado of bakers.

Looking over my shoulder I debated joining them at the movies.

Dad began cleaning up the eclair mess as I started in on where Sacia had been working. Trying to sort through the morning, I realized I'd forgotten something. "Wait, what was the news about where Ms. Pie In The Sky was planning to build? Was it Chicago?"

"No, sources say she's heading in this direction, towards Madison."

My stomach dropped at his words and I gazed around my bakery with images of the monster of Milwaukee coming to tear my dreams away.

Chapter 8 — Mirror, Mirror, In The Field

Sacia

When I woke up, the sun was low in the sky. I knew it was early, but I didn't care. We were going to camp today, heading out to meet a bunch of new people, and hopefully having a ton of fun.

We made sure to sign up early so we could all be together. The camp offered a bunch of different morning activities. I mostly wanted Horseback Riding, though Archery would be fun too. There were six options and we had to rank them from first to last. As long as I didn't end up in Field Games, I honestly didn't care. I guess I didn't want Cooking Delights either. I spent enough time at the bakery, I feared what they'd try to 'teach' me.

Somehow the camp officials had lost my applications and Gramps had to make some calls. In my opinion, my preferences should be moved to the top, to when my original application had been submitted. Only time would tell ... and that time was today. Chills of excitement ran up and down my spine.

Last night, I spent the night at my best friends' place, Charlie and Pris. Though their parents had offered to let them have their own rooms, they still shared. They decided they'd separate when they got to high school. Their current room had a bunk bed with a pull out. This allowed the three of us to each have our own place to sleep.

I quietly scooted from the bed and headed to the bathroom. We always stored our outfits there so we wouldn't wake the others up when we rose.

I washed my face, brushed my teeth and hair, then got dressed. My hair was short, so I ended up needing to wet it down to get it to stop trying to salute the ceiling.

For the first day of camp I wore shorts and a light blue t-shirt Gramps had made for my birthday. It had a cupcake on it and said, *'You cake handle all of me!'*

The cupcake was one of his specialties. I loved it.

When I opened the door, Pris was there. She saw the shirt and smiled. "Perfect! I'll meet you downstairs."

In the kitchen, Mrs. Weber stood leaning on the counter drinking coffee. "I'll have a bagel and scrambled eggs ready in a jiffy. Do you want orange juice or milk?"

Usually, I'd go for the juice, but I thought with being outside all day, like Mom always said, the milk may carry me longer. "Milk, but I can get it. Thanks."

She nodded and started up the stove to make the eggs.

As I got the milk, I said, "Pris is in the bathroom. I don't know about Charlie."

"She's down here. There was a line and she couldn't wait."

It didn't take long for all of us to be eating. The three of us couldn't sit still with camp on our minds.

Mr. Weber walked through. "You kids are vibrating the house. I didn't even need an alarm to wake up!" He laughed at his own joke, before grabbing a soda and joining us for breakfast. "I'll take the girls to camp. Rosy said she'd pick them up, feed them, and bring the twins back."

Mrs. Weber nodded. "Sounds great. I have a long day at the firm. We have a new customer, but they're in California and want a late afternoon meeting. That translates to after three, probably later. With the two hour difference, it will start after dinner. I don't know how late it'll run or when I'll make it home." She drooped. "I love my job, but boy it can go late."

He leaned over and kissed her forehead. "At least you don't have to drive to Madison anymore. That forty-five minute commute wasn't bad, except on days like this. You'd get home so late."

"That's true. The fact that there's a remote office here in town is fantastic." She smiled. "It gives me a lot more time with the girls."

Pris's brow furrowed. "If you're working late, does that mean you can go in late as well?"

Mrs. Weber chuckled. "You'd think, but no. I also have a client in Ireland. They are six hours ahead of us. They wanted to meet during the morning, but nine in the morning for them is three a.m. for us. If I can get there by eight," she checked her watch, "which reminds me, I should go!" she sighed. "Then I can at least make the meeting an early afternoon one. They knew when they signed up with us that we are American based and that any morning meetings would take a lot of finagling."

Mrs. Weber gave each of us a hug and ran out the door.

We all watched until the door clicked, then finished our meals before cleaning up.

At the new camp, the councilors asked that parents drop the kids off and leave. They didn't need parents parking and performing any long good-byes. That suited everyone in the Weber car just fine.

Once the car ahead of ours finally departed, I unclicked my belt, gathered my stuff, and prepared to hop out. I wanted our car to be the most efficient in the lot, despite having three campers to dispatch.

"Okay girls, have fun, do your best, remember your families love you, and above all, have fun."

Charlie grunted. "You said that last bit twice, Dad."

"It's important." He stopped the car and the three of us leapt out, clearing the way for the next car.

A counselor sat at a table, ready to check us in. "Name?"

"Charlotte Weber"

The woman's pencil dragged down to nearly the bottom of the list. "Oh, there you are. You'll be in the Horseback Riding group. Follow the path over there. It's a bit of a hike to the stables, but once you get over the hill, the way is pretty obvious."

Charlie moved to the side to wait for us. Our hope was we'd all be together.

"Name?"

"Priscilla Weber"

Again she started at the top.

Why didn't she notice two people with the same last name and just assume she'd need the other one's placement? I'd have thought that would be obvious. Maybe they don't hire these people for their smarts. I worked at not rolling my eyes.

"Oh, you're right after Charlotte, I guess I should've realized you two have the same last name. Are you two sisters? You don't look alike." Her head tilted as she asked the question.

"We're twins." Pris said tightly.

"Ah. Okay, well, you're in the Archery group. If your aim is as sharp as your tongue, you'll do great!" The woman smiled. "Same path as the Horseback Riding group. Once you get to the top of the hill, turn right."

I hope she isn't anywhere near Pris with a bow and arrow. She did not make a friend today.

Pris stepped over to Charlie. Neither of them looked thrilled.

Before she could ask, I said, voice flat, "Sacia Roads." *Please let me be with one of my friends. Please let me be with one of my friends.*

My mind kept chanting the words as, once again, the woman started at the top of the list. *Doesn't she know how the alphabet works to search for my name?* "You'll be in Field Games." She smiled wide. "You'll be heading over that way." She pointed in the opposite direction from the way the twins would head. "Just around the corner there's a huge field. You can't miss it."

Disappointment filled me, heavy and sharp. I wasn't going to be with them at all until after lunch.

I trudged over and gave each of them a hug.

"It'll be okay," Pris said, a small smile on her face. "You'll go and be brilliant, I'm sure of it."

Charlie nodded. "It's because your application got lost. You're so amazing, you'll make a million friends, and by noon, the two of us will be jealous."

With a shrug, I slung my bag over my shoulder and headed in the direction the woman had indicated. I knew that this was camp and the point was to have fun. Whatever we did would be better than sitting indoors all day. And the twins were right, I would make new friends.

That is, unless everyone took one look at me and decided to hate me. Kids are awful, there is never a reason.

The field was as easy to spot as the new counselor standing with a clipboard. I approached him and noted he had a name tag that stated 'Craig - Field it in your bones!'

The smirk played across my face without my bidding. I was annoyed with this placement, despite his punny humor.

His eyes darted up to me for barely a second. "I already told you, over by the hula-hoops. Did you get lost?" The annoyance and frustration in his voice wasn't lost on me. He sounded like he was done with idiots. I knew that feeling.

Spinning on my heel, I shrugged. Voice tight, I said loudly enough that I figured he'd hear. "I just thought I needed to check in. Sorry if I was wrong. If not, the name's Sacia. Last name Roads." As I sauntered away, I heard his sudden intake of breath, but ignored it.

Across the field there were seven other campers who had, or maybe had not, checked in. This camp had people from several towns nearby. I didn't expect to know many, if anyone, in attendance. As I approached, I thought I may know a boy from my school in the group, but I wasn't positive. Standing closest to me was a girl with hair a similar color to mine.

Is that still enough to bridge the gap to friendship? Or are we now too old for such trivialities? Gah! Getting old sucks.

One of the other camper's eyes widened, then, mouth agape, she tapped the girl with the blond hair and pointed at me.

About five to ten feet away, the girl turned, and chills prickled my body. It was like looking into a mirror. She looked exactly like me ... except her hair was a bit longer. My head tilted to the left and I squinted, trying to see if there were any differences. My mirror image's head tilted to the right and squinted.

It was weird.

Hair, clothes, beyond that, I couldn't see anything else different. She was exactly the same as me.

What the hell?

I licked my lips ... so did she. My eyes widened. So did hers. As I squeezed my fists to hold back my influx of emotions, I saw hers tighten. Before she could react, I said, "I'm Sacia."

That broke whatever it was between us. She shook her head quickly and a small smile played across her face. I knew that smile. "Gilly." There was a moment of silence, then her brows knit as if trying to figure things out.

My smile stretched across my face. "Sacia. Are you adopted? Like from the bus crash?" Shivers ran down my spine. *It couldn't be. Charlie and Pris were the twins ... right?*

Craig's voice boomed from behind us. "Alright everyone, partner up, we have a day of fun in the sun ahead of us."

Gilly and I launched at each other. There was no way we weren't going to spend the day trying to figure this out.

Chapter 9 – The History Of Pekara

Nora

There were six cars ahead of us in line. It surprised me when I learned that the parents couldn't park and bring their kids up to the camp, but looking around, the parking lot wasn't huge.

It probably speeds everything up, too.

"Are you at all excited for your first day of camp, Gilly?"

She shrugged, forehead leaning against the window looking out. "I guess. I mean, I don't know anyone, so it'll be weird. What if everyone here knows each other and they all hate me? I'll be all alone?"

Reaching out, I patted her knee. "It won't be like that, and you know it. From what I read, this camp has campers from about a half dozen or so schools, maybe more. It pulls from a few different towns. You'll be fine. Not to mention, you are amazing."

She flopped back, gazing up at the roof of the car, and sighed. "Yeah, okay. I won't be the only one who doesn't know everyone, but I'll be the only one from Milwaukee."

"You don't know that, and, if anything, it'll make you seem mysterious and cool."

"Ma'oom! God, no one talks like that!"

I smiled. "I do, now go!" I quickly leaned over to give her a hug and a kiss on the forehead before she pushed out of the car.

As I pulled away, I saw her trudge slowly to the check in desk. There were a few kids ahead of her, and one of them turned to talk with her. I relaxed as I saw her smile. *She's going to be okay. Camp is always fun.*

I gave myself a block to worry over Gilly, then headed into town. The main street of Pekara could be painted and hung on a gallery wall as quintessential America. The parking was all diagonal, and once I'd found a spot, I gazed up and down the street. At the corner there was a diner. Fe and I agreed to meet for breakfast and to discuss plans for our stay.

As I entered, Fe ran up behind me. "You got here just before me. How was Gilly's drop off? Was she excited? Annoyed? Devastated?"

A teenager met us and led us to a booth. "Coffee? Water? Sodas?"

"Coffee, please."

Fe nodded. "Me, too."

I opened the menu and did a quick search, despite its size. I knew what I hoped it had, and I was mostly doing a search more than reading. Once I found it, I shut the menu and folded my hands atop it. "My daughter was apprehensive. She worried about going into a camp where she didn't know anyone, but I have confidence in her."

"Agreed, she's amazing."

Two coffees were placed on the table. "Do you know what you want?"

My eyes snapped to Fe and she nodded. I shifted my gaze to the server. "I'd like a sausage and egg skillet. Eggs over easy and a side of sourdough toast, please."

"Sounds perfect, and for you?" The server collected my menu and turned to my assistant.

Fe opened the menu, looked at it for a moment, then faced the young lady. "I'll have the chocolate chip pancakes with a side of bacon."

"Excellent choice, it's the kitchen's specialty." She tucked Fe's menu under her arm and smiled wide. "I'll have those orders up right away. Will you need anything else while you wait?"

Her chipper attitude made me smile. "I'll want more coffee in a few minutes, and if it isn't too much trouble, a couple of glasses of water."

"Not at all, I'll be back in a sec." And then she was off.

Fe smiled. "Small town charm." She shook her head. "Do you ever long for places like this and how nice everyone is?"

I leaned back. "A place where everyone knows who you are and is in your business? I think I can do without that."

"Oh, it's not that bad." She sipped her coffee, grimaced, and added more sugar. "I'm sure there's such a thing as privacy."

One of my eyebrows shot up. "I don't think so, but we can ask Delia."

Once the food came and we'd had a few bites, I asked, "Where do you think we should start?"

"Do you want to check out your competition? Stop by the bakery?"

I gaped at her. "After eating those things, you want more sugar?"

She ducked her head and smiled, then took another large bite of her pancakes. "Can't help it, they're amazing. Maybe it's something in the water ... or air."

"No, I don't want to go there today, maybe tomorrow or later in the week. We should get some chores done first." I ticked things off on my fingers. "City hall to genuinely get a feel for tourism, numbers, fluctuation throughout the year, you know, the facts and history of how this town runs. If all that goes well, I'd like to see if there are any places we could buy or rent. I didn't see any signs in the windows, but maybe we can get the down low somewhere. Lastly, we should see if there are any Italian or Thai restaurants nearby. I want to be prepared with Gilly's favorite foods."

Fe nodded as I spoke. "Okay, once we're done eating, let's head back to your place and get organized, maybe do some searches. Then we'll go to city hall, see if anyone will speak with us."

"Sounds like a plan."

"And we need to be at the camp by four thirty." Fe reminded me.

"That is definitely on my mental list of to do's." A smile slowly crossed my face. I liked having a plan for the day.

The line for picking up the kids was much longer than the drop off. Not having a set schedule right now, I debated coming early and just waiting in the future. I knew I should spend some time doing my normal day job, but I liked the idea of having a week or two of semi-vacation.

Despite the length of the line, there were a few counselors who helped to keep the line moving fast. At one point I thought I saw Gilly getting into the wrong car, but then I realized the girl's hair was too short, and the clothes were all wrong.

Get a grip, Gilly isn't going to go home with the wrong person, not to mention, three kids got into that car. The exact situation Gilly worried over, groups who knew each other before coming. I wonder if that group was so tight knit that they were mean or excluded others.

The door opened, jarring me from my thoughts, and Gilly slid in, her eyes twinkling. *Thank goodness.* "Hi love! How was your day?"

"It was ... okay." A smile spread across her face. "Thank you for sending me, it was way better than I thought."

A light joy lifted some of my guilt for forcing her to leave her friends this summer. "So, not a camp overrun with farmer's kids?"

"Ma'ooom! Just ... no. I mean it. There were some ... other campers, they were fun." After a pause in which she gazed out the window, she shrugged. "We got along."

"So, tell me about it. Did you get the session you wanted?"

"I did, I was in Field Games. We partnered up. I met a girl before the activities started. She was ... I like her. We had an egg run—"

"Did you win?"

"Mom! I'm telling the story. And it's me, do I even have to answer that?"

I chuckled. "I guess not."

"Then we went on a scavenger hunt in the woods. It was so fun. Sa—, my partner and I were good together. I know we just met, but it was like we could read each other's minds. We were totally in sync. Then we had lunch and there was a full camp session. We had to stay with our mounting groups ... you know the first group we're assigned. We learned about nature and how things are preserved for when people come to visit."

"Like the nature preserves?" I wasn't quite following this part.

"Yes, and the hiking trails, and everything." I could feel her gaze, so I nodded my understanding. "Once we had a better understanding, we went out to help clear the trails so that when people go out hiking, the brush and weeds don't trip them. We also picked up litter."

The more I hear, the more this camp impresses me.

Gilly shimmied in her seat. "Some of the campers come on a scholarship. They're signed up for the full summer. Every other week they spend the morning session doing more intensive work in the parks and woods. Things like pruning the trees so they stay healthy, painting fences, things like that. They get paid a bit, but they also don't have to pay the other weeks and they get their first choice of activity."

"Would you have wanted to do that?"

She shrugged. "Yes and no. I like where I ended up, the other campers in my group, but I love the idea of learning more about nature and helping to keep things healthy and safe."

We drove in silence for a few minutes. Then my daughter got still. I quickly looked over at her before driving the last block to the house we'd rented. She looked pensive, almost anxious.

"Gilly, you okay?" I parked, but didn't immediately open the door.

She shook her head. "Yeah, I was just wondering. Did you know that the bus crash ... you know, *that* one. It happened around here?"

Every muscle in my body tensed. "The one which brought you to me?"

Her eyes rolled loud enough to hear. "Yes, Mom, that one. How many bus crashes could I be talking about?"

"I did. I thought we could talk about it this summer." Her questions felt like a punch to the gut. *Were there other kids at the camp that knew? Were they still talking about it? Was another one of the kids from the accident there?*

She bit her bottom lip. "Could you tell me about it?"

Where was my sassy daughter? "What do you want to know? I've told you the basics."

She shrugged. "Do you know how many couples were on the bus? How many kids? How many survivors there were?"

I rubbed my face. "You've never seemed interested before, love, you've never even asked."

"I know ... I'm just. Someone at camp mentioned that the bus crash happened near here, near town. It got me thinking about the other kids from the crash."

Dread chilled me. Does she want to find her 'real' family? Does she think I'm not good enough? Shaking my head, I took a deep breath to try to calm myself. "We can go inside and look it up, if you'd like."

Gilly's face lit up and she swung her door open. "Thanks Mom!"

"After dinner!" I yelled after her.

We had enchiladas that Delia's family had made. She'd been with them for the last few days. She hadn't seen them for a while, and looked relaxed and happy to have had the time with them.

Once done, we headed to the computer. We found an article that stated seven couples had been on a pregnancy retreat. They all were due within a few days of each other.

Gilly perked up. "Whoa! So all the kids were due on April second?"

"Well, on or around, love." I kept scanning the words, trying to get all the important information. "They were all early April babies. There had been a late March blizzard and the roads were still slick. Apparently a deer ran out and the bus driver swerved, lost control, and the bus flipped."

Imagining it made my stomach churn with bile. All that life lost because of a freak accident.

Next to me, Gilly looked ready to cry. "Did anyone survive?"

"All of the babies did." I wrapped an arm around her. "Should I stop? This is pretty heavy stuff."

"No, it's just weird to think I was on that bus ... I was one of the survivors." She shivered. "How do they even know about the deer and stuff?"

"The bus had a camera, and the bus driver survived for a bit after the ambulances arrived." Looking over that article and a couple more, it amazed me how little I could find. "Besides what I've told you before, the hospital and child services sent the kids into foster care. They could only find biological relatives for some of the kids."

"Do you know how many?"

"No, love. That isn't in any of the reports."

"Do any of them mention twins?"

My eyes widened and I tried to speak for a few moments before words actually came out. "Twins?" Gilly nodded. "Really? Did you meet a set of twins that survived the crash today?"

My daughter wrapped me in a big hug. "They're nice. I like them. And well, I like all the people I met. Thank you for bringing me here, Mom."

Chapter 10 – A Mile A Minute

Rosy

Monday morning, I got to the bakery early. There were several regulars who came in to get boxes of goodies for early morning meetings and I loved to gossip with them. The third variation of cookies were in the mixer when Dad lumbered in. "Morning Rosy, I'm just going to grab some coffee and I'll be right back there."

We worked in silence, baking and filling the store's cabinet until I needed to open the store. Almost immediately, the bell chimed with the first customer.

Dylan gazed down at the display, searching the options. "It all looks good, but I need something to win over the masses."

"You work at a factory, why do you need to butter up your workers?"

He sighed. "There have been complaints of migraines and other headaches."

"I mean, machinery is loud, right?"

A genuine smile spread on his face. "Yes, but these are complaints of artificial scents ... you know, from body sprays and perfumes."

Without thinking, I groaned. If I worked there, I'd be complaining, too. Dylan nodded. "Right, you see my issue. Well, in today's staff meeting, I'm going to tell everyone that those things are not to be allowed anymore at work."

"And you think you'll be stepping on some people's toes."

"I do."

"Well, we have all our usuals, which I know you love, but we also have some trays of brownies over there along the wall." I waved at my new addition.

His eyes widened and he went to see the new selections. He ended up with the brownies and a box of cookies, including the Sacia special, eclairs, and cupcakes. "Your new offerings are very exciting, Rosy. I'm sure everyone will be thrilled."

Later that afternoon, a woman came in who I didn't recognize. She looked harassed and tired. "Can I help you?"

After rubbing her eyes, she nodded. "I'm sorry, I just, I'm from a town over. My ex works in the bakery there and I crave a fruit tart." She scanned what we had, and slumped.

I reached in and selected a Red Velvet cookie and handed it to her.

Her eyes widened. "I didn't order this. I—"

"On the house. You look like you need it."

Hand trembling, she took a bite, and moaned. "Oh God, this is fantastic. I was wrong, this is what I needed. I think I've died and gone to cookie heaven."

Chuckling, I waited as she took a second bite. "So, what did this ex do that makes you feel the need to avoid them?"

"She tore the labels off all the cans in my pantry. Now, I didn't know where each can was, not exactly, but I did have a sense. I knew the soups were to the right and the black olives to the left. Well, it didn't take long to realize she's moved everything around, too."

My jaw dropped open, and the woman nodded. "But that's not all, she took all my spoons."

"Your spoons?" I know I sounded dubious, but I couldn't fathom the logic behind that.

"Yeah, my spoons. And my shoelaces." One of my brows popped up as I didn't know how to respond. But the woman just continued, not noticing my silence. "Shoelaces. Like, how do you think of doing those things?"

Finally, I found my voice. "It sounds like you escaped a real doozy there."

Eyes widening, she nodded. "Yeah, I truly did." A smile spread on her face. "A dozen of these and a large coffee, please."

Just after four-thirty, the three girls dove into the car like a herd of sheep baa-ing, and donkeys braying. Almost impossible to understand.

"Whoa! I don't know what you're saying when you all jabber at me at the same time."

I navigated out of the parking lot and made my way towards downtown. "Does the diner sound okay?"

They all cheered and then the car got eerily silent.

Since we were close to the diner, I decided to just be happy with the lack of a need for ear plugs for a few seconds.

Once we were seated and everyone had ordered, it was time to decipher their stranger than normal behavior. "So, did you each get your preferred choice?"

Charlie shrugged. "Yes and no. I did get Horseback Riding, but since the other two weren't with me, it wasn't as preferred as it could be."

Pris nodded. "All three of us were split up. It was second grade all over again."

"Yeah," Sacia nodded as waters were placed on the table. "I ended up in Field Games."

I groaned. Her last choice of options. "Was it horrible?"

Her mouth opened then shut, a look of indecision on her face. "It was camp. They always find ways to make things fun ... even when it's your last choice for an activity."

"Wow, look at my little lawyer go!"

After a moment a smile broke out across her face. "It isn't that, it's just that, even though Charlie and Pris were off doing better things, there was a new camper in the field activities. She's nice. I like her."

"And does this new friend have a name?" A warmth filled me that Sacia was branching out. Over the years, the triplets had avoided expanding their friend group, relying on each other for all their social needs. The idea she'd met someone new, someone who wasn't an April second baby, was amazing. It made me feel all giddy inside. I couldn't wait to tell the others about it.

Charlie smirked. "I had fun learning about the horses. Today we got to choose the one we'd care for over the summer. We learned how to brush and care for our new friend, including cleaning their feet."

Pris's brow furrowed. "That's it?"

"It's more than what it sounds like. They want to make sure we know what we're doing. We can't do the fun without knowing how to care for the animals who will carry us."

"I think that's wonderful." I said, wanting to support what the camp did. "Are you also learning about feeding your mounts and cleaning their pens?"

All three girls made faces and squealed in disgust. "Mom, are you bringing up poop while we're trying to eat?"

"No, I think you're the one who did that." I chuckled.

"Well, that's just gross."

Still laughing, I turned to the last of the three. "What about you, Pris, where did you end up?"

Her eyes lit up. "I got Archery. I know we all signed up for horses, but I think I'm glad I ended up where I did. Learning to shoot a bow and arrow is a life skill I can use."

My mind boggled at where and when she thought she'd be shooting a bow and arrow, but I just shrugged. "Did you do theory today or did you get to let the arrows fly?"

"We did a lot of theory, but the counselors said they'd intersperse theory with practice. We got to do actual play. And, it was amazing." She tapped her chest with both her hands. "I was amazing. I was one of the only campers to hit the target. If this continues, I may ask Mom and Dad to set something up in the backyard and continue my lessons. It's just so ..." Her voice trailed off as she gazed off into the distance.

Sacia leaned forward. "It's an Olympic event, you know. If you get good enough, you can win prizes."

All three girls' eyes widened as their smiles got calculating. Then they descended on their food as they devoured what was in front of them.

Once done, I took the twins home. Their mom had to work late again, but their dad was home and ready for them.

The drive home was quick, and collapsing on a couch, Sacia looked tired. We watched one of our favorite shows, recorded from the night before, then called it a night. She'd head into the bakery with me in the morning and Mr. Weber would pick her up on the way to camp. Getting to sleep early was important.

As I tucked her in, she stretched. "Mom, do you know how many couples had been on that bus before it crashed? How many kids? Were they all adopted like me, Charlie, and Pris?" She yawned and curled into a ball.

Leaning down, I kissed her forehead. "I don't, but we can get some if not all those answers tomorrow."

Her head bobbed. "'K. Thanks Mom, I love you."

"I love you, too."

As I headed to the kitchen for Chamomile tea, I shook my head. She hadn't asked questions about the bus and the other babies in years.

I wonder why the sudden interest.

Chapter 11 – Fancy Meeting You here

Nora

It was so much nicer to drop Gilly off on Tuesday. She seemed excited to get to camp and see her new friends. The fact that she *had* new friends so soon after the camp started thrilled me. *I just hope this is the start of a great summer for her! And who knows, this town isn't that far from Milwaukee, any friends she makes here have the potential to continue later.*

The car had barely stopped, and the click of the seatbelt echoed in the car. "Bye Mom, love you, see you later."

As she ran off, I tried to see if I could pick out anyone specific she ran towards, but she followed a path and disappeared.

Oh well, I'm sure I'll meet these friends eventually. Either they'll come over to our place or she'll want to go to theirs. Either way, I'll have to learn something from my closed-mouthed child.

My first appointment for the day wasn't for a couple of hours. It was time to size up the enemy.

It wasn't a good idea to think of the other bakery as the enemy. From everything I'd seen, this town was probably big enough to support two shops. Moreover, the current bakery specialized in cookies and cupcakes, two items my shops weren't known for. If I worked with the current shop, maybe we wouldn't even be in competition ... at least, not too much competition.

Once again, parking wasn't bad. At dinner the night before, Delia had told me she'd spoken to her parents about Road's Café and Bakery. According to them, it was a town jewel. Even though it'd only been around for twelve years, everyone spoke of it as a town landmark.

I don't know if opening up a competing bakery would go over well with the locals. I shook my head and got out.

Opening the door, a small bell chimed pleasantly. I heard some talking in the back, it sounded like a man and a woman—a couple?—and then a tall, slightly rotund man walked out wearing an apron covered in the evidence of his baking. "Good morn—" his eyes narrowed. "I know you."

"You do?" This both surprised and didn't surprise me. As hard as I worked to keep my face and private life out of the public eye, both for me and Gilly, a few images did leak out, especially in the highly select bakery rags.

"You're Elenora Shifer, owner of Pie In The Sky and Heavenly Delights Bakery chain out of Milwaukee. I recently read that you were planning on opening up a shop in this direction, I just assumed you'd pick a town without a thriving bakery." He grunted. "Are you really planning on coming here to Pekara?"

"Mr. Roads, I assume. Is this how you treat all of your customers?" Annoyance surged through me at his attitude.

"Dad, what's going on out there? Do you need me to cover?" The woman in the back called as the sound of running water stopped. I wasn't sure she'd heard any of our conversation.

"It's fine, I have this. I believe this *customer* was just leaving." His lip twitched as he watched me.

Not reacting to his words or attitude, I continued to stand, gazing back. "Actually, I would like to buy a few items."

"If you don't want to work the counter, I'll take over. I think your timer—" The woman stepped through the doorway and my breath caught. It wasn't just any woman, it was her, the birthday woman from the bar, Ms. Turning Thirty-Seven. My world turned on its axis, and I suddenly felt queasy.

This can't be happening.

I missed part of what she said, gazing at the cookies in the display as my mind tried to figure out how the curvaceous knock-out from the bar could be the same person working in the kitchen here. Maybe the man owns the bakery and she—the daughter—just works here. Maybe she's just helping out. Maybe ...

No, none of that makes sense. From everything I've learned, a woman owned the bakery, not a man. A woman. And her dad helped out.

My hands trembled. Why? It had only been a chance encounter, what did I care that she owned the bakery? What was wrong with me?

Forcing myself to straighten, I gazed into her eyes, and saw my confusion mirrored back. "Nora?" Mutely, I nodded. Her mouth pursed, then she nodded. "What would you like to order?" She sounded all business. There was none of the fun person from the night at the bar.

"Rosy, can we talk?"

"I'm at work. Apparently a business you want to close down. I'm not sure why, or what we did to you or yours, but," she shrugged. "For now, what do you want to order?"

This wasn't how it was supposed to go. "It's not like that."

She shook her head. It looked like she was barely holding it together. With a sigh, I waved. "Two each of the Red Velvet, Italian Rainbow, and Snickerdoodle." I narrowed my eyes at the Italian Rainbow cookies. "What do you mean by the Sacia special on those?"

"If you must know—"

The bell rang as more customers came in, laughing. "Rosy! I'm so glad you're already at the counter. We need some cookies and cupcakes, stat!"

Her face transformed when these townspeople came in, and my heart ached for her to smile at me like that. I threw a wad of cash on the counter, more than what my order cost. She'd finished boxing up my baked goods, so I grabbed my purchase and left. I didn't want to get in the way.

I decided to save the box for Gilly. At least watching her pick through the sugars would bring the joy back into the treats.

Chapter 12 – And Another Thing

Rosy

Making cookies brought me joy. Finding new ways to combine familiar flavors was always exciting to both me and my customers. This town's support was at first shocking and now ... smiling at how much I loved hearing their stories, baking them cookies, and serving them coffee, I couldn't even imagine doing anything else with my life.

I was working on my third variety of cookie when Dad showed up to start on cupcakes. The display was full when Cindy texted. *The birds are aloft.*

On mornings like this, when both me and the twin's parents were super busy, I don't know what we'd do without her.

The bell rang and I went to meet the customer. I didn't recognize him so I smiled. He looked a bit scared. "Can I help you?"

His eyes darted all around the store before landing on the baked goods in the display and then on me. "Um, I'm here on behalf of ... um, Melody?"

With an effort, I kept my smile small. There was no way I'd keep a blank face. This must be the new guy Franco had brought home. "Did Melody say anything else, or just that she wanted her regular?"

Somehow, his eyes got bigger. "She just said to go to the bakery and the woman behind the counter would know what to do."

"Sounds great." I started to fill a box. "How is work at the library? Are you enjoying it?"

"What?" He stepped back, searching the walls and ceiling for something. Maybe a camera or other recording device? "But how did you know?"

His fear was going to kill him. "Whoa! Here is your order." I gave him a total, and he pulled out a credit card. "Cindy is my best friend. No one is watching you, I promise."

He sagged. "Sorry. Ever since I got here, everything is so weird, you know. The new job is great. Cindy is really nice. But, I don't know what the others in the house expect and I'm afraid to ask. It's a great deal, but what if they kick me out."

I shrugged. I couldn't solve everything. "Good luck, Callen."

He laughed humorlessly. "Thanks."

Before I could get back to my cookies, a man slammed through the door. "I need your help, it's an emergency."

One of my brows rose. *Your emergency buster, not mine. And since when is that the appropriate way to enter a place of business, you almost ripped my door off its hinges.* In lieu of saying any of that, I smiled. "And, what seems to be the issue?"

"It's my anniversary tonight." I just nodded and waited. "Like, the twenty-fifth anniversary."

"Congratulations." *He's had a person in his life for that long, and I can't even get a date. At this point, if I ever do find someone, we'll be dead before we have a twenty-fifth anniversary.*

"I need a cake, you know, something that will make my wife swoon ... and not kill me."

Locking my jaw, I rubbed my face. This was the type of order that required twenty-four hours, not, I checked my watch, seven. "There are signs up that state our twenty-four hour policy. They are clear on the website as well, sir."

"I know." He sounded pained. "But, it's an emergency. I'll pay double. I'll pay up front. What can I do?"

Before I could answer, Dad put his hands on my shoulders. "What flavor cake does your wife like and how big of a cake? We have options over there in that book."

The man scurried over and I twisted to glare. I hissed out low, "What are you doing?"

"If he's willing to pay double up front, why not? We can be flexible, considering we're ahead in all of our work. You're saying 'no' on policy, not timing. You can get the cake done in a few hours."

Breathing slowly, I mentally cataloged everything we needed to do today and tomorrow. With Cindy taking Sacia to camp, I got well ahead on my work. Dad was right, even if I didn't want to admit it. As long as he didn't select the hardest cake, we should be fine.

"Um, she likes chocolate, and vanilla, and, um, sweet things?"

Dad spun me. "Go start pulling ingredients. I'll figure this out."

I realized he was right. The man frustrated me and Dad would get the order from him faster. In the kitchen I selected what every cake needed, flour, eggs, sugar ....

Dad came in with the exact cake the man needed and the time he'd be in to pick it up. "Oh, he chose the cake with the most eggs, but whatever."

In reality, I'd have found something to complain about no matter what and Dad knew that.

Half way through cracking eggs, the bell chimed again. Seeing my predicament, Dad nodded. "I got it."

"You sure?"

He chuckled. "Yeah, you with eggy hands is not the best look."

"Fine!" I said in a teasing voice.

I quickly finished and went to wash my hands. As much as Dad didn't mind the customer side of the business, it wasn't his favorite part of working in the bakery.

There was some tense talking. "Dad, what's going on out there? Do you need me to cover?" I wanted to get the egg mess cleaned up if I could, though it sounded like he needed me to get out there, fast.

"It's fine, I have this. I believe this *customer* was just leaving."

Huh? I hadn't heard the cash register. What is going on?

In a flat voice, the customer responded, "Actually, I would like to buy a few items."

"If you don't want to work the counter, I'll take over. I think your timer—" Words stuck in the back of my throat. Standing in the middle of my bakery was the woman from my birthday. She wore a similar outfit and in the bright lights of the store looked just as good.

God, I must look horrible, I've been baking all morning. Do I have flour in my hair? Egg? Is there icing on my face? How awful do I look?

Words from her conversation with Dad solidified in my head. I hadn't paid attention because I didn't think it mattered, but now ...

Opening up a shop in this direction ...

Pick a town without a thriving bakery ...

For fuck's sake! Nora was Elenora Shifer, the fucking CEO of Pie In The Sky! What was she doing here? And why had I played tongue wars with her?

The bitch was casing my store. I wondered if she was evaluating every item in the display as she stared daggers at my variety of cookies. *Does she think she can do better? She can't. Mine are the best.*

Despite my bravado, I wasn't sure.

Her eyes finally lifted to meet mine. She looked ... nervous. Was the woman from the bar somewhere in there? "Nora?" I wanted to kick myself for being a fool, of course she wasn't. She said she wanted to order something, well, I could be professional. "What would you like to order?"

"Rosy, can we talk?"

Hope warred with the reality of the situation. I had to be strong, for me, for Dad, and for the girls. "I'm at work. Apparently a business you want to close down. I'm not sure why, or what we did to you or yours, but," I shrugged trying to hold in all my emotions. "For now, what do you want to order?"

I was shocked at how calmly I spoke despite the cage match battling out in my gut.

Her eyes widened a pinch. It was barely noticeable, but I'd obviously struck a nerve. "It's not like that."

I just couldn't. Not here, not with Dad listening in. My body trembled with the need for this to be over. Finally, she waved. "Two each of the Red Velvet, Italian Rainbow, and Snickerdoodle."

Relief flooded me that she finally selected something. I was surprised she hadn't chosen any cupcakes, I thought she'd go for variety.

"What do you mean by the Sacia special on those?" She tapped the window as I boxed up a couple of the Italian Rainbow cookies.

I didn't want to share any more of my life. She'd gotten more than enough at the bar. But, I'd rather not make a big deal and let her know she'd gotten under my skin. "If you must know—" the bell chimed as the door opened.

Saved by the bell.

A group of high school kids walked in. "Rosy! I'm so glad you're already at the counter." The leader came up to stand by Nora. His name was ...

Timmy, Tommy, Bart, Martin, that was it, Martin! "We need some cookies and cupcakes, stat!"

I smiled wide. Teens were always so overly dramatic. "Is the play going well?"

"Yes, but we need sustenance to make it through rehearsals."

The bell chimed, and I saw Nora heading down the street with her box. There were two one hundred dollar bills on the counter. *Fuck.*

"Hold on Martin." I called over my shoulder. "Dad, I need you up here."

He came up and I quickly explained. Then I rung up Nora's order, made change, and ran after her.

"Hey!" I yelled down the street.

She stood by a dark green car that looked fancy. "What? I paid."

"Too much, I have your change."

"You can't take a tip?"

"Do you think we're desperate?" The deed made me so angry, I could feel the heat warming my cheeks.

Her face tightened and she shook her head. "Or, I could just be trying to be nice. Give you a tip. The store didn't have many customers."

"You saw it for a couple of minutes. There are other times when we're buzzing with activity." My nails bit into my palms with how tightly I made fists. "Or do you think those two minutes were the end all be all of how my business runs?"

"I don't know. My bakeries tend to have people in them in a constant stream."

At her claim, I laughed. I couldn't help it, the lie was either her own ignorance by her own people trying to make her feel better, or something worse. She waited. "When was the last time you went to your stores, Mrs. Shifer? Because when I was in one a few weeks ago, to buy a treat and coffee, then sit and wait for—a friend—to be done with her appointment. I'll tell you, there was not much traffic."

I wasn't sure why I didn't want this corporate shark to know I had a daughter. It wasn't like everyone in town didn't know. I guess I felt she lost the right to know about me when she turned out to be my biggest competitor.

Again, she didn't have much of a poker face as the shock washed over her face. "Were you checking out the competition?" She sneered.

"No. I was getting a fruit tart, and as I said, waiting on someone." *It's not like I've ever thought of you as competition. Maybe if I repeat that enough, I'll even believe it.*

Disappointment played across her face, fast enough I almost missed it. "Thank you for the change, Ms. Roads. With a town this small, I'll be seeing you."

"Does that mean you'll stop competing with my bakery?"

"No, but remember, I don't think it'll be a competition." Her smile was down right lupine. "Until next time." She gave a small bow and, getting into her car, drove away.

Chapter 13 — The Start Of A Plan

Gilly

It had been five days, and I couldn't believe how amazing this small town was. I hadn't told mom about Sacia and the twins. She would try to get more information about the other bus kids, and I wasn't ready for that. I just wanted to get to know my new friends. Thinking about the gang, I held back a snort, like Charlie and Pris were the twins.

Every time I thought about what must have happened at that hospital, I was equal parts amused and annoyed.

I have a twin sister!

The car stopped at the head of the drop off line. I unbuckled and gathered my stuff as quickly as I could. "Love you, Mom." I hopped out. "See you later!"

"Love you, too!" Her words were swallowed up by the sounds of camp and the door swinging shut.

I loved my mom. She was smart, strong, and powerful. Despite being a single mother and a powerhouse who single handedly opened a bakery then franchised it; she also made sure to spend time being a Mom. There was never a time I didn't feel like a priority.

The thing was, I didn't think she tried to make friends outside of me, her assistant, and Delia. *Soon I'll be old enough to not need Delia around all the time. When I'm always hanging out with my friends, Mom will be home alone. I worry she'll get lonely.*

Will she ever find new friends? Date? I'll probably start dating before her!

As I did every morning since camp started, I turned towards the activity field. Ahead of me, I saw a group of campers whose names I didn't know heading in the same direction.

What are they doing? Are they lost?

When I got to the field, instead of seeing my counselor and regular group, it felt like everyone milled about. Scanning the mass of people, I finally found Craig and jogged in his direction.

"Sa-no Gilly. You two!" He chuckled. "Okay, we're waiting on a few more, and our group will all be here."

"What's going on?"

"It's Friday! Instead of doing separate activities, we get to do full camp challenges. We want the campers to know more than just the people from their one specialty. We're completely separate in the morning."

"What about the afternoons? We've been together then." His attention snagged on something behind me and I looked to see Sacia and the twins enter the field. Excitement built in me at seeing my new friends.

"Right. But those were us versus them. We want this to be more of a mixing of groups. We'll encourage you to join with campers from the other specialties today, not just stick with those of the best group." He winked, then looked down at his board to check in Sacia and the boy walking behind her.

Sacia linked her arm in mine, and we headed deeper into the field.

"Do you know what this is about? Beyond being a madhouse?"

I laughed and told her what Craig had said.

Once everyone had arrived, Sonya, the camp director, got our attention. "We need all of you to get into groups of four or five. We have an obstacle course that will take you all over camp. The more you diversify your group, the better off you'll be."

There was no question in my mind who our group would be. Once we had the group, we ran up to the nearest counselor and got the challenge.

Pris had the paper. "Oh, this is great. It's a series of challenges and questions." She snorted. "Oh no! We didn't choose anyone from the kitchen, what ever will we do?"

Sacia rolled her eyes. "What do we need to do?"

"It says, 'In a series of steps, follow carefully true, something sweet will be made, for me and for you.' It's obviously about baking something."

The other three laughed. I bit my lip. "I take it, you three know how to bake?"

We'd talked some about our past, but not a ton. I knew Sacia's mom owned the local bakery, the twins' mom was in marketing, and their dad worked as a nurse. I could understand Sacia knowing how to bake, though I couldn't, but the others?

They all nodded. Charlie tilted her head. "Don't you? Your mom owns, like, several bakeries, right?"

"Four."

"Have you ever helped out?" She continued.

I shook my head. "No, baking isn't my thing. Usually, I avoid anything that involves mixing ingredients, if I can." I thought for a moment, "Except for the shows. I love watching the shows. Those people can be idiots ... and hilarious."

As we spoke, we headed in the direction of the kitchens. The building was large, bigger than one of Mom's shops on the outside. Inside, the room looked like a science lab, with huge tables down the center, five rows of two. Each table had a setup of what looked like a drawing of a stovetop and basic ingredients. Along the walls were ovens.

When we got there, Charlie whistled. "Look Pris, it's one of those fancy setups like at the fondu restaurant. When the stove gets hot, it'll only warm up the skillet. It won't burn us."

"Cool."

My mind stuttered at the idea.

Walking up to the center of chaos, Sacia held out her hand for the recipe and quickly mixed up whatever was on the card. When she asked for something, Pris grabbed it.

Charlie shrugged. "All three of us help Sacia's mom out at the bakery. It's great."

The chef looked over Sacia and Pris's work. To me, it appeared to be a pretty perfect stack of five pancakes. Once the skill was checked off our card, Sacia smirked, "That was fun, not as fun as cookies, but I haven't had as much kitchen time this week."

Pris wrapped her arms around Sacia and smiled. "Agreed. We'll have to take over tomorrow. Kick both your mom and Gramps out."

They laughed and my gut clenched. These three accepted me into their group, but they'd known each other for years, and I'd only been hanging out with them for a handful of days. In reality, I didn't know anything about them or vice versa. *What if they decided they hated me.*

Next we headed over to Archery. *Okay, I'm not so bad here. I won't be an idiot this time.*

This challenge was set up to be a bit tricky. Two campers had to hit a target ten feet away. Charlie sat down hard. "Don't look at me. This is all Pris."

Sacia's mouth opened then closed, then she shrugged. "I've never tried. No idea."

My confidence soared as I wrapped an arm around both Sacia and Pris, my smile grew. "I got this one. Archery was my second choice."

Pris whooted. "Come on Gilly, let's show these two how it's done."

The practice field was similar to how it was set up in gym class. There were hay bales with targets across the field and six stations for the shooters. We had to wait for one of the stations to open up. The teams ahead of us weren't great.

Just like track, but now there are a group of us, ha!

When we got to take our turn, the counselor blew a whistle, then waved a flag. Everyone stopped. "Arrow clean up." He pointed at Sacia, Charlie, and four others. They all got up and ran to gather the arrows strewn all around. Then they helped to restock.

The whistle was blown again. "Begin."

Pris went first. She took a moment to take aim, but her first arrow hit the ring just outside of a bullseye.

I patted her back. "Nice! You have excellent form, too."

She blushed. "Thanks. I'm really enjoying this." Her face scrunched up as she gazed at me. "Do you know how to do this?"

"Yeah, we have archery at school."

Her jaw dropped. "For real? That's so cool."

I took the bow and arrow, took aim, breathed, and loosed the arrow. Everything about this setup was different from what I was used to, and the arrow went wide. Nodding, I rolled my shoulders, took a deep breath, and reset.

Next to me, Pris was saying something, but I had to focus. The sounds around me faded as I concentrated on just me and the target.

Setting up into position again, I made a few slight adjustments. From how the arrow flew, this bow was strung tighter than the ones at school. That made sense with how abused those were. That camp's setup was also longer.

I lowered my aim, shortened my draw, breathed in, and released.

The arrow landed on the line between the bulls-eye and the next ring. Tendrils of joy and excitement tingled within me. I lowered the bow and leaned it against the hay barrier in front of me. Then Pris practically tackled me in a hug. "That was amazing! You're so good at this."

The others joined in and I could've soared.

We slowly made it through the next few challenges. As we went, Pris said, "You know, Gilly, if you had shorter hair, the two of you would be impossible to tell apart."

Sacia shook her head. "Not true. We're completely different."

I laughed. "Oh? Do tell, mirror-me."

"That's just it, we're mirror images. We part our hair opposite of each other, and if you haven't noticed, you're left-handed." She shivered, as if that were an awful thought.

The twins laughed.

Charlie wrapped an arm around her. "Only you would notice such things, my friend. Only you."

With a huff, Pris went on. "If Gilly cuts her hair, then the two of you could swap, get to know each other's lives. Maybe you could see what it's like with each other's moms. I mean, you'd have to spend the next week genuinely telling each other everything, but," she shrugged, "what do you think?"

I stopped, eyes wide. "A weekend with the two of you? Wait, wouldn't that be easier?"

"No." Pris demanded. "Then we'd have to explain everything to your moms. That would lead to ... god, adults will make everything so complicated. This would be a lot easier. Trust me."

After thinking about the article I read, and what would happen if Mom found out Sacia was my twin, I realized, yeah, Pris was right. Mom always tried to manage everything, and I didn't know what she'd do—pull me from camp, try to make our lives harder, who knew—Adults totally made things harder than they needed to be. In the end, I didn't want to find out.

Gazing at the faces of my new friends ... my new family, I nodded. "Yeah, okay. I'll see if I can get my hair cut this weekend. Maybe I can get your picture Charlie. Tell the person I want it to be like yours."

Charlie smiled wide. "That's brilliant!"

"We won, we won!"

"Slow down there, champ, don't you always win?"

I danced in the car seat. "I know, but this was a full camp competition and me and my new friends, well, we won. It was amazing!"

"Will I ever meet these new super-star friends?"

"Ma'oom!" I rolled my eyes. Parents were so nosey. I began telling her about everything else we'd done during the week, hoping to distract her. Then I asked her about her week .. and that worked. She really wanted to start something new in town, which worried me because Sacia's mom was some sort of baking super-star that everyone loved. "What about the bakery that's already here? The cookies were so good."

She just shook her head. "Let's talk about something else. Is there anything you want to do this weekend? Do you want to tour the ice cream factory?"

I laughed. "Yes, of course I do. But, I was also thinking of cutting my hair. Would that be okay?"

Her mouth dropped open and her eyes went saucer-wide. She looked like a cartoon character. "Gillyflower Shifer, what has gotten into you? For years you've wanted nothing but to grow your hair to your ass—"

"Mom!" She never swore in front of me.

"Sorry, your butt. And now you want a haircut? What has this camp and these new friends done to you? Are there drugs involved?"

I wasn't sure if I should be appalled or amused. "Mom, no. I just ... it's hot, and my hair is getting in the way. It occurred to me, I don't need long hair to be pretty. I was being dumb."

She smirked. "Okay, I'll speak to Delia about finding a good place and we can go next week."

"You don't think we can find a place this weekend?"

"What's the rush, sweety?"

It occurred to me that next week would work as well as the weekend and I shrugged. "I don't know, I just like coming up with an idea and then doing it right away. Next week is fine." Excited, my voice rose. "Thanks Mom!"

The pleasure in my voice reflected on her face, and I realized I'd been snapping at her a lot. Maybe this trip was good for both of us.

Chapter 14 — But I Like Horses

Rosy

The girls were so loud when I gathered them from camp on Friday. The sounds were happy sounds, but ... I needed ... something.

Sacia twisted to face me, eyes wide, smile even bigger. "Mom, can I spend the night at the twins's place?" I opened my mouth to agree, but she went on. "We'll be at the bakery to help, you know we will, and, no, we're not sick of each other, it's just—"

"Stop," I interrupted with a laugh. "Save your arguments until after I give my opening answer. Ms. Lawyer extraordinaire."

She leaned back into the car seat, the tension growing in the car. "Okay, what *is* your answer?"

I took a slow breath, trying to prolong their suffering. In the end, I was a good parent after all. "Have you asked their parents?"

All three hooted, and I wanted to cover my ears, but couldn't because I was driving. The one saving grace was everything in town was close, and it didn't take long to get the three out of my car.

As always, I drove home and parked. My life was a series of predictable actions. It was simple, comfortable, easy. Every morning I woke up and went to the bakery. *God, I love my job!* Creating new baked goods resonated with me. Having a seven day a week job was hard, but with Dad it was doable.

After the third year, when we'd started making enough to truly be solvent, we hired a high school kid to help us part time. He was great. When he left for college, he said his younger sister could take his place. Loved that. We didn't even have to interview anyone. It happened again when she went to college.

When the third sibling left, we hit the end of the family's reserve of kids. We'd spent most of the last year managing well because we had the trio of twelve-year-olds in and out to help bake and when I needed a break. When they weren't around, Cindy could cover the store.

In the end, I knew all of these measures had been a band-aid. We needed to hire someone who could make the bakery a priority. Someone who could relieve either me or Dad. Maybe even two somebodies.

I shook my head, what was I doing? Sitting in my car outside the house? With a sigh, I slid out and trudged up to the door. Once inside I imagined one more night in a string of a million nights alone in this empty house.

Why don't I live for anything but my bakery or Sacia? Cindy was right. Dad was right. Hell, even Sacia has been pushing me to do more.

Moving fast before I talked myself out of my decision, I showered to remove a day of bakery from my body and hair, slipped on a yellow sundress layered with a black over piece that had sunflowers on it. The top tied behind my neck. It hugged my curves and flared when I spun.

A quick run to the bathroom to apply makeup and fix my hair ... *good enough. Who am I trying to impress? Tony?* I shook my head and laughed. *And off to the bar.*

The music beat through me, mixing with the three drinks I already had. Everything was starting to seem ... fuzzy. *Why don't I do this more? I feel amazing.*

Despite how free I felt, how pretty the dress I wore could be, I sat in the far corner of the bar, deep in shadow, hidden. In the back of my mind, I knew this wasn't how to meet people, but I was still in Pekara, and there was no way I'd meet anyone here. From what I gathered, the only other woman around who liked women was *her* and there was no way.

Elenora freaking Shifer, the bitch who wanted to close my bakery down!

"Did you say something?" Tony leaned close. "Do you need another? Maybe some water? I don't know that I've ever seen you drink so much, Rosy. And Cindy isn't here."

My eyes narrowed as I tried to glare. "She's not me keeper." Ha! I could still speak in sentences. "Why is there picture of horses?" I pointed.

His face scrunched up. "It's a drink."

My eyes widened. I liked horses. "Oh! Want!"

Lips pursed, Tony shook his head. "I don't think so."

"But I'm the customer. Why not?" Anger surged through me. Well, bubbled gently on a sea of blissful indifference.

"It's a drink called the Four Horsemen, and I'm starting to think I should have customers sign a waiver to drink it. It isn't for you. Not without a chaperone."

I finally got my glare working. "Tony, I want horse drink!" I didn't even know what it was, but I liked horses, and I felt like doom and gloom had come to town.

Maybe this is my rationale for avoiding the bar. I don't mix well with mixed drinks. I snorted at my funny. If I remembered any of it, I'd tell Cindy. Hopefully I wouldn't.

A glass was put down in front of me. "Pay first. I fear once you start in on this, you'll be done for. Someone will have to carry you home ... probably me."

I rolled my eyes, then regretted it.

Once my tab was closed out, I picked up the drink and poured about half down my throat.

It burned. My arms began to tremble. Setting the glass down, I heard a whimper, and worried it came from me. For a moment, or several moments, I just sat and gaped at the glass, wondering what I had just put into my body. My already hazy thoughts became a thick fog and I could no longer make any sense of anything.

"Is she okay?"

Do I know that voice? It makes all my muscles want to sing and flee at the same time. That's some superpower. All I have to do is look over there.

I tried to get my eyebrows to lead my face in the direction I wanted to look, it wasn't working well.

"I don't think so. She demanded one of these and she hasn't moved since slamming back half of it." Who was Tony telling my business to? It's private!

"My business!" I shouted. Or was it a whisper? Had I spoken at all? Do I still know how to speak? Is speaking even a thing?

"What's in it?" Gah! That voice again, it *did* things. It made muscles deep down clench, ones I didn't even know I still had ... could still use.

"Well, it's the Four Horsemen, Jim, Jack, Johnnie, and José." Did Tony sound tired?

"Jim Beam, Jack Daniels, Johnnie Walker, and José Cuervo." Her voice got hard. "And a shot of each? Was this at least her first drink?" I wanted to purr, curl into the voice. It sounded like it would take care of me and make my worries go away. Did I know it?

"Actually, a large shot, like one and a half, and no, it was her fourth, but I did try to stop her." Tony sounded like Sacia when she was making excuses. I huffed out a laugh.

The other person made a sound of disgust. "You're the bartender. You could've put anything in that glass. Why not vodka and sprite? Do you think she'd have known the difference? How often is she in here?"

"Honestly? This is probably her second visit in the last decade or so. Ever since she adopted that kid of hers."

My body tensed. *Why is he talking to somebody about me? What right does he have?* "Stop!" I hoped it came out louder.

An arm slipped around my back. "Did you say something?"

"Stop." I said with more force.

"Stop what?" She was close enough her breath tickled my cheek.

"Me. Talking. Stop."

"You don't want to talk?" Her confusion annoyed me.

"No. You. Tony. Me. Talking. Stop." Why didn't she understand?

Again, there was silence. Then her hair tickled my cheek as if her head shook. "I'm not sure what you're trying to say. But I think you need to get home, lovely lady. Tony, do you know if it's far? Did she drive?"

"Probably not. She lives a couple of blocks. If she knew she would be drinking, I bet she walked." There was another pause and I debated pulling away, but her arm felt so good. "I could call Cindy, her best friend. It isn't that late."

"If you trust me, I can take her."

"What?" That was it, Tony was going to give a stranger my address? I forced my body to listen to my demands and look.

Oh God no! It was *her!* Fucking Elenora Shifer. And my betrayer of a body reacted like she was candy. And she had her arm around me. I tried to pull away, but only managed to sway.

Four-fucking-Horsemen!

"Yeah, sure. I can point you in the right direction. Saves me from doing it at the end of my shift," said Tony the Betrayer.

"No. I'll make it." I croaked out.

They both laughed. Apparently, I got those words out clearly enough.

Unable to stop it, I listened as the two planned out my demise. Then Elenora Fucking Shifer tucked herself under my arm and all but carried me out of the bar.

Once we got out, I pushed away. I could walk just fine. I stumbled and fell on my ass. My confidence in myself was wrong. "Why is ... you?

You want ... destroy me!" I could feel the tears burning my eyes. That was the last thing I wanted.

"Come on, Mrs. Drunk, you can yell at me, but why not do it in the car? Fewer witnesses."

My head flopped to the side and I squeezed my eyes shut. I knew there was something wrong with the question.

Don't get in cars with strangers? *But I know her.*

Just walk home? *But I'm so tired and the world is spinning ... rude, by the way.*

I felt her manipulate me, but couldn't decide if I should fight or give in. Her hands sent happy tingles everywhere, and I giggled.

Her voice tickled my ear sending shivers down my spine. "What's so funny, sexy?"

Wasn't that word ... wrong? Should I be arguing? I was supposed to be yelling at her. I shook my head. I had to clear it. There was a click and I realized I sat in a car. "How ... get here?"

She laughed from next to me. "You are wasted. How did you expect to get home?"

I sighed. "Home. Sounds ... nice."

The heat of her hand returned, making me giddy. It rubbed up and down my leg and I shivered before relaxing back in the seat with a low moan. "Nice hand."

My eyes shut for a second ... only a second, but when they opened it was dark, and I was in bed. Alone.

Was that a dream? Did any of that really happen?

Chapter 15 — You Scream …

Nora

As I moved around the kitchen making breakfast, I wondered if Rosy was okay. It wasn't like I had her number, or we were friends. In reality, the woman hated me. The only reason she trusted me at all last night was that she was too drunk to know what was going on.

A smile crossed my face and I blushed just thinking about her. I didn't know what it was about this woman, but I wanted to find out. After first meeting Rosy on her birthday, I liked how we got along and wanted to explore possibilities. But now …

But now she hates me.

I loaded two plates with sausage, hash browns, and eggs. Placing them on the small kitchen table, I refilled my coffee and poured a glass of orange juice. "Gilly! Breakfast!"

With all the energy of a twelve-year-old, she appeared as if by magic, sliding into the chair and almost slamming into the wall. "Morning, Mom." Her words were breathy, like she'd run a marathon.

"You okay there, champ?"

She smiled. "Yeah, I was just texting with my friends. I guess ... well, it's a weird day for them this morning. I'm not sure why."

This didn't sound good. "Is everything okay?"

Her face scrunched up, then she nodded. "Yeah, I'm sure it'll be fine. It's just ... I may be on my phone a bit more than normal. Only to monitor this situation."

On the one hand I loved that Gilly had friends, on the other, tweens could be so dramatic!

"I was hoping we could go out and do something today. Would that be okay?"

"Like what?" She stilled, gazing at me.

I pulled out my phone and searched. "There are several things in the area. We could probably get tickets to tour the cheese factory. There's also a chocolate factory." She perked up at that. "And of course, the ice cream factory." I continued.

Her eyes narrowed. "That's the one you want, isn't it. It's not just a mother daughter thing, it's about business." She glared at me, all the pep gone.

Not even the scent of coffee could lift my spirits in the face of such child scorn. "I said you could choose whichever one you want. I can tour the ice cream factory at any time."

Leaning forward, face pinched, eyes narrowed, I could feel the ire pouring off her. "So, if I demand the chocolate factory, you wouldn't fight me?"

A bit disappointed, I shook my head. "No. The point is spending the day with you, not the where or the what."

One side of her mouth quirked up. "Okay, good. I'll get dressed, then we can go."

"Okay, I need to get tickets and then clean up. Also, I did find an appointment for your hair. We can go on Tuesday."

Gilly turned and gave me a smile. "That's great. I can't wait." Though her words were positive, her eyes dimmed a bit and her hand lifted to stroke her locks.

We can always cancel the appointment and hair grows back.

"So, we can get in at the chocolate factory at ten or two, which would you rather? Before or after lunch?"

Her head bobbed back and forth. "Let's do ice cream." Her smile practically took over her face as she spun and darted off to her room. "I just wanted to make sure I was still your first love."

I rubbed my temples, realizing I wouldn't be able to keep up with her as she hit the teen years. I found an eleven o'clock tour of the ice cream factory, texted Delia to see if she wanted to join, and reserved three spots.

In my room, I searched for clean jeans and a t-shirt. This may be my normal weekend attire, but since coming to Pekara, I'd dressed this way just about every day. I was running out of outfits. Searching, I wasn't sure if I'd end up in something business casual or run around town naked. After finally unpacking my suitcase and sorting everything I'd brought, I found a light purple sundress with a black belt.

Good enough!

The drive to our destination took just under twenty minutes. As we pulled up, Gilly said she'd received a text from one of her friends, and everything had been resolved.

I didn't know the details, but I was happy for her and the unknown 'friends'. I hoped one day to meet them. Maybe then I'd get more details. *Ha!*

Delia met us there. When Gilly saw her au pair, she squealed. "You didn't tell me Delia would join us!" She leapt out and ran to her friend and gave her a big hug. "Oh my God, I have so many things to tell you. You will not believe what this week has been like!"

"Oh?" I asked. "More than what you've told me?"

"No!" She said spinning. "I've pretty much told you everything. You know that." For some reason, I doubted she told me as much as she told Delia. *I'll have to get used to knowing less and less as she gets older. It's hard seeing my baby grow.*

Delia wrapped an arm around Gilly's shoulders. "I bet you've had a great week. I told you this town was the best."

My daughter beamed up at her. She beamed! After all the guff she gave us, now she was all smiles and rainbows. *Have I ever understood that kid?*

Shaking my head, I led the way in for the tour.

"If you want to sample some of what we make, follow the green path to where we sell a few of our products. If you feel you're all ice-creamed out, take the dangerous red path, but that's the wrong choice." The kid, maybe seventeen, gave us a goofy smile at his joke, "It leads back to the parking lot." He waved at the two paths. "And don't forget, our flavor of the month is huckleberry white chocolate chunk. We get the berries wild and fresh from Montana."

He waggled his eyebrows before waving us off.

Gilly clenched my hand in hers in a vice grip, then dragged me down the green path. If I didn't follow, I feared for my arm.

Delia followed, softly chuckling.

The room where they sold their ice cream wasn't like a normal ice cream shop. There were a couple of standing freezers with a selection of maybe five of their most popular flavors. Another teen stood behind a counter with a blackboard behind her. It listed all the flavors she could scoop from a case in the back.

Gilly searched. "Where are the displays so we can see what we're buying, maybe get a taste to know if we like it? Where are the images of mouth watering ice cream to excite the senses? This isn't like any ice cream shop I've been to."

"And you've been to plenty." Delia murmured, much to my delight.

Instead of being annoyed, Gilly's smile widened. "Exactly! I'm an expert."

Her assessment and word choice showed she was an expert in marketing as well. It amused me how quickly she summarized my impression as well.

Resting my hands on her shoulders, I gave them a quick massage. "Now do you see the full picture?"

She leaned back and relaxed into me. "Yeah, I do. I think it's rather brilliant, really. I'm surprised it hasn't been done. Are you going to speak to people here?"

"I'll set up a meeting, hopefully this week."

Delia narrowed her eyes. "What are you planning?"

"Not here, not now, but we can talk when we're alone."

Being as smart as she was, she nodded, allowing the matter to drop.

Once we left, we decided to head downtown to the diner for lunch. I saw Rosy and her friend in another booth and wondered if she was on break from the bakery or never made it in at all. Despite looking tired, she still looked lovely as ever. *Is the woman ever unkempt?*

Luckily, Rosy faced the opposite direction and didn't see me.

After our food came, the friend looked up, stiffened, and glared. Rosy seemed to miss the whole interaction. I was glad Gilly was tucked in behind Delia and couldn't see the animosity of some of the other people from town. I don't think my sassy daughter would've handled it well.

I guess I couldn't expect to be everyone's friend.

Chapter 16 — But I Need To Get To Work!

Rosy

My head pounded. It felt like it matched my alarm, but my alarm was never that awful. Nothing had ever been this horrible.

Am I dying?

I curled into a ball and wished for death.

Periodically I heard buzzing, but my alarm didn't make a buzzing sound, and if my alarm hadn't gone off, whoever it was on the phone could wait.

My body trembled with pain. My stomach churned. The room spun.

God, let me off this ride!

The pounding in my head got louder, reverberating down my body. If it got any worse, my head may literally crack open.

The light in my room turned on. "Gah. No. Why?" I tried to cover my face, but nothing seemed to work right and my arms shook.

A cool hand rested on my forehead. "Sick or drunk, my friend?"

I forced one of my eyes open, sticky with sleep-goo. "Yeah? Cindy? I think I'm dying."

"Hold on, let me get you water." She got up, and bless her, she turned off the light as she walked out.

I thought I heard her speaking with someone, but I wasn't sure who. When she returned, she forced me to sit up and drink. At first I recoiled, but then, the cool water felt like a lifeline.

"That's it, my idiot of a best friend. You know, when I told you to go out and live a little, I didn't mean go out to the bar and drink yourself silly."

"Didn't want to think."

"Yeah, well, how'd that work out for you?"

I grunted. She knew me well enough to know what I meant.

"Okay, you need to get into the shower, get dressed, and come with me to the bakery."

Her words all made perfect sense. "Work, right, on it."

"Oh no. Once you've shown that pretty face of yours, we'll go get breakfast. The girls are worried. Mitch, well, he guessed what happened, sent me over here to get you sobered up."

My face fell into my hands. I couldn't imagine facing them. Despite my reservations, Cindy man-handled me—woman-handled me?—to the bathroom. She forced me to shower, which, despite my expectations, did end up making me feel better.

Dressed in jeans and a t-shirt which said, *I'm only responsible for what I say, not for what you understand,* I trudged to the kitchen for coffee. It had never tasted so divine in all my life.

"Can you walk to my car, or do I need to carry you?"

One of my brows rose, but I knew her threat wasn't idle. She tossed books around for a living. To her, I was just one more stack to move.

The house still felt more like a houseboat than anything on solid ground, but as I gathered my purse and phone, I didn't let Cindy know. I worried what her next helpful set of ministrations might be.

In the car, I checked the phone. I had a slew of texts from Dad, Sacia, Cindy ... everyone. My head fell back and my eyes closed, just long enough for the nausea of being in the car to overwhelm me, forcing me to sit up and open my eyes.

I saw we were on main street and Cindy was about to park, *thank God!*

On the sidewalk, she hooked her arm with mine. "Okay, we'll just stop into the bakery long enough for the girls to know you're alive."

"Were they really that worried?"

Cindy scoffed. "You're always the first up, always working, always responsible. I don't know that they've ever seen you sleep in." She paused, making me stop ... which was good, since I felt we'd been walking a bit fast, and I liked that we were letting everything settle. "Come to think of it," she continued, "I don't know if I've known you to ever sleep in."

I grumbled. "Ha ha. Let's just move this along."

The bakery stop was blissfully short. The girls ran out to give me a hug.

Sacia's squeeze was extra tight. "Are you okay, Mom?"

"I am. I just overslept. It happens to everyone." I thought I may keep a bit of my misbehavior from them. They were only twelve.

Dad came out from the kitchen and his booming laughter filled the space. "God, look at you. How much did Tony let you have last night before cutting you off?"

I gaped, unable to form an answer. Not only did I not want to, I wasn't sure. Moreover, I couldn't believe he asked in front of the girls.

Cindy rubbed my back. "She had four drinks. As to what they were, we'll talk about that later."

In an almost mirror of what I figured I looked like, Sacia's mouth dropped. "You drank last night? That's why you couldn't wake up?"

My mouth snapped shut. Then I opened and shut it a few times, trying to figure out words to say, but nothing formed.

Dad chuckled. "Girls, Rosy is an adult. If she decided to have a few cocktails, that's her prerogative. The fact that it took her twelve years just means she didn't know what she was doing."

Sacia's face hardened. "But Mom, I had something I needed to ask and if you're not working today, you *won't* take tomorrow off."

The pounding in my head ratcheted up a level.

Dad's voice softened, probably seeing me wince. "What did you want, Sacia?"

"The bookstore in Kenosha, the one I love. Studio Moonfall. It's having one of its book festivals tomorrow, and one of my favorite authors is going to be there. And the newsletter mentioned a surprise."

Sacia read so many books, and my poor pickled brain couldn't dredge up the list of her favorite authors. "Which author?"

"Mom! A.R. Grimes! I can get signed copies of all the books I love. And it's only like, I don't know, close enough."

Cindy said, not being at all helpful. "If you can get stock made in the morning, I can cover the store. You'll only be gone a few hours. Go, get the books, and come back. Mitch can restock as needed. Right?"

Dad nodded. "Sounds like a plan to me. And we're talking about encouraging these girls to read."

My head made thinking and planning impossible. I made a few sounds and gestures and finally Cindy pulled me out, guiding me to the diner.

Once we had coffee, and a second cup of coffee, and some water, I ordered a burger and fries.

Across from me, Cindy glared at me. "Okay, friendo, you've been keeping secrets. What has happened that caused you to drink the Four Horsemen?"

"How did you know?"

"I called Tony, you idiot. Now, no changing the subject."

While we ate, I told her about Elenora Fucking Shifer, her plans to run my business out of town, oh, and how she was the same hot woman I met on my birthday.

"She's what?" Cindy shook her head.

"I know. So freaking sensual ... and tempting. And her kissing, I could melt just thinking about it." My head hit my crossed arms and I mumbled into the table. "Why am I fantasizing about a woman who wants to destroy me and the business I've created. My life? What kind of masochist am I?"

"Damn, that must have been some kiss." Cindy reached over to rub my arm.

I looked up, meeting her stare. "I can't be falling for her. Dad would disown me. Hell, I would disown me."

Cindy's face softened. "Okay, you need to be distracted."

"I do, tell me something to get my mind off of," I waved my hand, "all of this."

For a moment Cindy's face scrunched up, like she wasn't sure what to say. I took a bite of my fries, enjoying every bit of their salty goodness. When she didn't say anything, I narrowed my eyes. "Have you figured out Selena's cat's name yet? Is it Cutie Squish? Kitten Pie? Little Beanie Toe Cutie Patootie?"

Her gaze darkened before she laughed. "I haven't. The cat is great. The idiot orange beast, I swear it never gets the communal orange cat brain cell."

"The what?" I knew my own brain needed drying out to be at full capacity, but I had no idea what she meant.

Laughing, her face lit up. "You are such a feline luddite, my friend. If it isn't sugar related, you have no idea. You should spend some time over at Lawrence's Books and Cats across the street. Not only can you relax and read, the cats are all amazing."

"He always has scratches up and down his arms." I countered.

One of her brows shot up as she sipped her coffee. "He is the happiest person in the whole damn town, is what he is." Amusement radiated from my friend. "Orange cats are known for being ... well, let's just say less than the brightest of the bright. The joke goes, they all share a single brain cell, and they pass it around." She shrugged, eyebrows high. "I just don't think our ... Marmalade? Cheddar? Mango-Pop? Nori-roll? Ever gets it."

"Wow, I would not think you'd just eaten with that list of names. Still hungry?"

Her eyes cut to the side and her mouth pursed. "Naw, we should go. You need to plan your great adventure to Kenosha for tomorrow, my friend."

A shiver ran down my back. "A whole weekend away from the bakery?"

"You'll go in and spend a few hours restocking the cookies. I know you. But yes. It's been open for twelve years. This shouldn't be that much of an oddity. You should be hiring more help."

"The hiring process is just so ... gah!"

"I'm going to take you home. Take a bath, relax, try to detox, maybe even read ... you remember how to do that, right?" Cindy teased.

"I do." Rubbing my face, I thought about my bathroom. "I wonder if I even have bath stuff."

Cindy sighed and, after throwing bills on the table, dragged me up. "Hardware store, then home."

"Right. Chuck's place has everything."

"It does now that Mildred helps out." She laughed.

Even though the hardware store *had* everything, it didn't mean finding it was easy. We spent several minutes searching the aisles to find bubble bath. Cindy insisted on a shelf that went across the tub as well for any bath distractions and two candles for the counter. "Look, you can get cookie-scented!"

With a groan, I searched until I found a non-bakery inspired scent.

After paying, we laughed at what the candle makers thought of as 'cookie' scent, as if there weren't dozens of different cookies. Distracted, as we walked out the door, we ran into *her*.

Part of my brain screamed I should remember … something. I just couldn't. "What do you want?" I snapped.

One of Elenora Shifer's eyebrows rose. "It seems you're doing better than last night."

Cold dread chilled me and I wrapped my arm through Cindy's. "Let's go." I nearly dragged her to the car.

As we drove away, Cindy's head shook. "Was she at the bar last night?"

"Um, no?" The pounding in my head returned and it brought friends.

"You don't sound sure."

"Cindy! When you found me did I look like a person who remembered much about last night? I don't even remember getting home. God! What if she drove me home?" My face fell into my hands. "My business and now this. Utter humiliation. She's probably laughing her ass off at me thinking how easy it'll be to destroy me." My mind flashed to her … a heat built low as I thought about how her dress clung to her curves. *Gah! Stop it brain! She's the enemy, she is not attractive.*

Cindy's warm hand rubbed my shoulder. "This town loves you, Rosy. No flashy big town *anybody* can waltz in here and take that from you. You know that."

As fear washed through me, a thought followed in its wake. *I wish my confidence in me was as strong as hers.*

Chapter 17 — An Ally, Maybe Two

Nora

Gilly ran into the living room. "Can we go to Main Street again? Have breakfast at that diner? Delia said the breakfast food was the best. And since camp happens all week, this is the only day I can do it."

Checking my watch, it was earlier than my twelve-year-old usually awoke. "You're volunteering to be up before seven-thirty? Who are you and what did you do with my daughter?"

"Ma'ooom! If I waited, you'd have started to cook. I had to get up stupid early." Her eyes widened and she gave me a huge smile.

"Fine, but I want to check out the stores, and if we're having breakfast, you're going with me. No sitting at the *Books and Cats* shop reading and making me go around alone."

"Promise!" The word was out almost before I could finish speaking.

With a grunt, I pushed myself up and headed to get dressed. I'd done laundry and had options, but still debated shopping for more casual wear this week. Another pair of jeans or light summer dress would be nice.

Gilly bounced by the door when I finally emerged minutes later. "What took you so long? Adults are so poky!"

Another glance at my watch informed me I'd taken roughly six minutes. "Well, you know it's hard to move these rickety old bones. Now, to the car with you, ya scamp!"

She dashed off, fast as the Flash. *That girl's speed is amazing. I'm glad she's going to be in that summer program in a few weeks. It'll be good for her.*

It didn't take long to get to the diner. *I'll miss this when we return to Milwaukee. Everywhere we go here is so close. Hell, we could've walked in less time than it takes to drive most places back home.*

I only spared a quick glance towards the bakery as I passed. The place looked warm and inviting, with the window displays showing cookies and cupcakes on one side and a three tiered cake on the other. Everything about the place made you want to go in and try whatever it sold.

With a shake of my head, I focused on Gilly. Alright, food and then a tour of Pekara's best.

The food at the diner excelled once again, and Gilly sighed with delight, patting her tummy. "Mom, I'll admit that you're a great cook, but that was so good. Okay, a deal's a deal, where to first?"

Across the street from the diner, taking up the corner location—prime real estate—stood Nita and Nikki's Nick-Nacks. That looked to be a great place to walk off our full bellies.

The store had five rows that towered high to the ceiling. Gilly and I each took our own aisle. Within minutes, the array of old and new sucked me in. Hidden on a shelf, I found cookbooks, some with titles of cooking shows, some that looked to be from the eighteen hundreds. Opening one, I dragged my finger down some of the ingredients and steps. A tingle of desire ran through me. *These would be so fun to try out. Too bad I don't have someone to cook with. I wonder if Rosy cooks savory.* With a start, I shook my head. *Why would she be interested in cooking the best of the best from the eighteen hundreds with me., She can't stand me.* I had to stop thinking about the gorgeous baker.

There were picture frames and kids toys, kitchen appliances, photo albums—some with old photos in them. Around a corner, I found another room with more towering shelves stuffed with items from centuries long gone. The weight of ages enticed me as I slowly walked deeper into the belly of this beast.

Some areas of the store had a thin layer of dust, as if people had forgotten its existence, or if the store had only opened the rows up for me, knowing these treasures would tickle my interest. I found toys and objects that reminded me of my childhood. Nostalgia hit and I walked slower.

"Finding everything you need?" A woman approached, maybe in her thirties? Sixties? Twenties? How could someone be ageless, like the wares she sold? Her head was shaved bald and her eyes sparkled with knowledge and joy.

"Yes, thank you. There are so many ..." Lost, I couldn't fathom how to describe what I looked at.

The side of her mouth quirked up. "Knick-Knacks?"

A laugh bubbled out. "Yes, exactly."

"Well, I'm Nikki. Just find me if you decide you'd like any of my shiny treasures. Nita and I are collectors, but we appreciate finding others who see the value in our goods." With a wink, she spun and walked away.

In the end, both Gilly and I found a couple of items that spoke to our souls. Gazing at Gilly's new doll, I hoped it didn't come to life at night. As for my cookbook, if I start making videos of me creating recipes from two centuries ago, would anyone watch? I bit back a laugh as Nikki bagged up our stuff. I don't know which of us was more excited. *If my videos go viral, I know who will be less excited!*

The next store over had a 'for-sale' sign across the window. I knew about this shop. It had been on my tour of possible ones to rent or buy. Then we arrived at *Rags To Riches,* an eclectic used clothes shop.

I didn't have much hope for this second-hand store. According to the sign, they didn't take random donations. They looked through what people were willing to give up, and only took the best. They sometimes altered the clothes before reselling it.

Gilly dashed into the massive store, searching. My pace was a bit slower as I searched for ... something.

A few minutes later, my daughter howled for me. As I approached, I saw she held up a sky blue dress with mushrooms on it. "Mom, this would be perfect for you while we hang out here."

I narrowed my eyes, but decided she was right. My daughter, my new personal shopper. The gremlin of a girl's ego soared and over the next few minutes she found a few more dresses for me to try on. Then she found a couple of sun-dresses for herself.

We asked for a key to the dressing room, then tried on each item. Gilly let me see her selections between each change. I nearly doubled over when I saw her in a psychedelic minidress with go-go boots. *Where did the boots come from?*

"All you need is a sixties updo."

Her eyes danced. "I know! This is great. I'm ready for spirit week *and* Halloween."

I snorted, then returned to the small changing room. In the end we got Gilly two dresses and the boots, and three dresses for me. As I paid, I realized how much fun I was having.

The next shop was the infamous *Books and Cats*. Gilly placed a hand on my arm and gazed up at me with large eyes. "I know I promised I wouldn't go in there, but I'm getting tired, and reading a chapter from my book while cuddling Boomerang would do me wonders."

"Boomerang?"

She smiled wide. "A white elder cat with a black splotch-like line from his hind leg to his neck. He's amazingly sweet."

A movement across the street caught my attention. I saw someone leaving the bakery and realized it wasn't Rosy behind the counter, but her friend. A stab of disappointment shot through me, but I ignored it. *I'll think about that later.*

Maybe her friend works for her? Maybe that's how they met.

An idea wiggled its way into my mind. It was probably a horrible idea, but I felt like a boat alone in an ocean here in Pekara, and maybe I could find a way to not be completely isolated.

Coming to a decision—probably a rash, idiotic, and fruitless decision—I smiled down at my daughter. "Sure. Let's get you settled with the bags. I'm going to visit a few more stores ... ones you may not be interested in."

Bouncing, Gilly bit her lower lip. "Are you sure? You're not mad?"

"Nope. Not at all. I get it. Lead on." I waved in the direction of the door.

A tall, dark brown man waved as we entered. An aura of welcome, contrasting the zippy disdain from the cats, came from him. His low voice vibrated throughout the store. "Welcome. How can I help you?"

"My daughter came in yesterday. She'd like to sit and cuddle with Boomerang and read a book on her phone, if that's okay?"

"Of course, I remember her. She came with Delia. I support all reading." He had a smile that was contagious.

Smiling back, I gave him a small nod. "I'll be around looking at some of the other stores. Gilly has my number if anything is needed."

"I don't think there'll be any issues at all." His smile stretched across his face as he waved to some couches.

"Thank you ... I don't think I caught your name."

"It's Lawrence. I'm known for books and cats around here. That and a mean grill when I throw a town pot luck. Have been since before this store. You can always find me near one or the other." Again, he bowed his head.

"Books or cats?"

"Or grilling." He winked.

"Nice to meet you." She held out her hand. "I'm Nora."

"Welcome to Pekara, Nora." His shake was warm and I felt a connection to the town I wasn't expecting.

I tried to hold on to his and Nikki's welcome as I crossed the street to the bakery. My mind filled with fingers pointing towards the door and scowls demanding I leave the premises. *'And don't come back, you devilish fiend!'*

Taking a calming breath, I braced myself before pushing open the door to the happy bell, which mocked me with its small 'welcome all—except for you, Elenora Shifer'.

Stop it! You've built your career on confidence. Don't lose your spine now.

The friend stood behind the counter. She had dark brown eyes and short black curly hair. As I approached, her eyes narrowed. "Welcome!" Her fake smile turned to a scowl. "Are you here to case the joint?" Her voice was barely more than a whisper and she kept looking over her shoulder.

Was Rosy back there? Could I get a chance to see the stunning woman, even if only to be kicked out by her? God, what am I thinking?

I licked my lips, knowing I had one chance to make this woman understand. "No. Will you give me a couple of minutes to explain?"

Her face pinched and one brow lifted. "Make it quick. And if an actual customer comes in, you're done."

There were sounds in the kitchen telling me we weren't alone, but I just needed one person attached to this bakery to hear me out. I nodded quickly. "Understand. I do want to expand out this way, but once I learned there was a bakery in town, and it was thriving, I didn't want to compete."

"Ha!" The other woman's face said everything. She crossed her arms across her chest and slowly shook her head.

I'm losing her.

"I'm good at what I do because I figure out what communities need. Pekara doesn't need a bakery. You have one. I want to do something different, something that could work with this shop, complement it."

Heavy steps came from the back and I realized the sounds from the kitchen had stopped. The man who I'd first met, Rosy's dad, came to stand by the woman. "And what exactly do you think would complement our shop? A coffee shop? We sell that too. Baked goods we don't sell? We try out different things each month, anything you sell would hurt our bottom line. No, Miss. Shifer, I can't see what kind of store you can open that would do anything but pull dollars from our books."

This was it. Either I convinced these two, and found allies, or I spoke with Fe about finding a new location and starting over. I didn't want to build surrounded by animosity and I was coming to love this town. "Mr. Roads, Miss ..." I shrugged, "I'm sorry, I don't know your name." The friend continued to gaze at me with a hard face. With a small shrug, I continued, knowing I'd built my life on fighting for my dreams. "As I said, your town has a bakery, as well as many other tourist attractions. What I want to do is capitalize on what is missing."

With a snarl, Mr. Roads snapped out. "We're not a committee you need to convince, just finish your spiel so I can get back into the kitchen."

"Right." I nodded curtly. "I want to open an ice cream shop." In unison, both their faces comically dropped. "You have the factory, but their post-tour store is awful, not to mention, there's no place in town to buy their 'best ice cream in the state'. I think if there was a shop that sold their ice cream as well as ice cream sandwiches ..." I shrugged. "It would be good for both businesses."

Mr. Roads leaned forward. "Where would the ice cream sandwiches be sold, your shop or ours?"

"Doesn't matter. It could be a commission either way with profits being split. Again, I don't want to compete, Mr. Roads. I'm convinced we can find a way to work together."

Next to him, the dark-haired woman beamed. "I'm Cindy, by the way, and I love this idea. I've wanted the Hernandez family to expand for ages."

"Well, getting a meeting with them has been tricky. We, my assistant and I, have been making calls, but they are a hard bunch to pin down."

The two behind the counter smiled. Then Cindy shrugged. "Let me make some calls after the bakery closes, I may be able to help." She looked between me and Mr. Roads. "One question. Can I ask you about Friday night, the bar, and if you saw Rosy there drunk?"

Heat burned in me thinking about that night. Anger over Tony's idiocy and desire for how beautiful Rosy had looked. "The idiot bartender served her a ..." I shook my head, trying to remember.

Cindy nodded. "Four Horsemen."

Mr. Roads swore. "The fuck was Tony thinking? Rosy never drinks. It's her second time in the bar in a dozen years and he gives her that?"

My brows shot up. The woman had been out so few times and I'd been lucky enough to catch her there both times? Either the coincidence ran high between us, or she snuck off behind her people's backs more than they knew.

The disgust on her dad's face both pleased me and reminded me of something I didn't have. My family was scattered throughout the state. I could see them, well one of them, but the easiest way was a bit ironic. Mr. Roads's devotion to his daughter was heartwarming, even when it meant he bristled at me. "Tony said she demanded it. She was already a bit drunk and said she was the paying customer. If she said she wanted it, he had to give it to her."

"No!" he snarled. "It's his responsibility to know when not to serve a drink."

"Heh." I laughed humorlessly. "I said something very similar to him right before dragging her home. I was pretty sure she didn't remember it.

Tony gave me her address because she barely knew which way was up, much less how to walk at that point. I think he was just happy he didn't have to keep her there until close and take her home himself."

"No." Cindy said sharply. "He was glad he didn't have to call me to bring her home. The ass." She crossed her arms on the counter. "So tell me, corporate woman, I saw you on Rosy's birthday. Do you actually like her?"

My mouth opened, then shut. Were we in middle school? What was happening? This felt oddly like conversations Gilly had with her friends during the school year. *'Do you like so-and-so? Should I tell them? Oh! Send a text asking if they like the same influencer you do.'*

"Is that any of your business?" I wondered if I could get out of here without answering.

Mr. Roads's head fell back and laughed. "I'll never escape these conversations, not for years! Will I?"

I had no idea what he was talking about, but Cindy smirked and patted his arm. "We live in a small town, Mitch, and your daughter runs the hub of gossip here in the bakery, so no, you never will."

Rosy hears all the gossip? Good to know.

He gazed at me as if he could read my mind. I didn't think people really could, but in this town I no longer knew. "If you do fancy my Rosy—and believe me, it would be nice if someone shook up her life—she'll be at the Thai restaurant tomorrow at twelve-thirty. Trust me, she needs a bit of a diversion."

"Siam Noodle?" I'd tried the place in my first week here. Living in Milwaukee with much better Thai food, it saddened me that that was what the people here in Pekara thought of as good.

"Gah! No way. Other side of town, Thai Spice. It's a bitty hole in the wall you'd miss if you didn't know it was there. She goes when I tell her it's a good idea and we can cover the store. She's had a rough week and I had planned on doing it. If you don't like Thai, it'll never work between you and my daughter, so, it's good to know now."

The laugh that erupted out of me, shocked me. "No, I like Thai. I like most things. Okay, Thai, just after noon. Got it. Thank you Cindy. Thank you Mr. Roads."

"It's Mitchel. Mitch to my friends. We'll know after tomorrow which one you are."

Chapter 18 — Portal To A Good Time

Sacia

The twins' parents dropped us off at the bakery mid-morning. There was the normal crowd of people all clamoring for cookies and cupcakes. Some came for coffee, others for gossip. I loved the bakery, it was my favorite place to hang out. Not just because Mom was amazing and baking was fun. It was the heart of town, and everyone knew it.

I want Gilly to come here and love it, too! She said my description sounded different from her mom's bakery.

Inside, Cindy was already there, covering the counter. "Morning girls. Rosy went home to shower and get the car. She should be here in a minute, then you'll be off to Kenosha for the book festival. I'm so excited for you."

Charlie bounced. "Me too, I mean, I know A.R. Grimes is there, and there was a promise of a surprise, but there should be other authors and book stuff, too!"

"Well, you know what I like. If you can find a book for me, you know I'm good for it." She pointed with her chin. "Your chariot awaits."

We all turned and saw Mom waiting in her blue Subaru Outback. We cheered, raced for the car, and were off.

The drive took just over an hour. When we got there, we saw all the festival booths that were set up in a parking lot across the street from the book store, Studio Moonfall. Chills of excitement danced through me like stars in the sky, as I pressed my nose to the window. Mom couldn't park fast enough.

Pris tapped her window. "Look, there's a food truck, someone who sells balloon art, and a place to do artwork. This is so amazing."

As we walked through the festival, we tried to speak with each of the authors. Some wrote books in genres I didn't like—horror and gore. Ew. There were some that Mom was interested in, like fantasy with romance. Gushy stuff. But finally, near the midpoint, we found a quirky author with an octopus hat. "That has to be the one!"

She stood next to another author with long brown hair. We ran over. The display had characters in armor and portals. The table was covered in dragons and toads, and I wanted everything.

"Hi! Are you interested in my books?" A. R. Grimes's wide smile pulled us all closer to the tables.

Mom came up behind us. "All three of them are. Sacia here got your newsletter and wants a full collection of signed books."

"A full collection?" The slight bafflement was evident, but the other author laughed.

"Of course they do, your books are lovely." As one, we all turned at her foreign accent. I'd never heard anything like that around here.

Mom sidestepped and picked up one of her books, dark with a bright red ring on it. *Legacy*

Bound by Elizabeth Daly. "I'm guessing you're not from around here," she said and began reading the back.

Unable to stop myself, I did the same.

The author chuckled. "No, I'm just here visiting several author friends. When this event popped up, I couldn't resist. I'm from Ireland."

My head snapped from the author to Mom. "We have to get this one, too. How often will I get the opportunity to meet, much less have a signed book, from an author from over there?"

Mom gazed at all three of us and sighed. "Do you two need any of the *Wyldling Dream* books? I know you love those, too?"

Pris shook her head. "We got them last time."

Shutting her eyes, Mom stretched her neck and stilled. "Okay, three of these, please. Sign one each to each of the girls. And how much do I owe you for the full collection?"

It didn't take long for the authors to sign our books. We also got bookmarks and stickers. Excitement burst in me at my collection of goodies. We headed to the tables near the food truck as Mom continued to search for some books for herself.

The two authors we'd just spoken to said that the rainbow haired author in the next stall had a large selection of queer romance. Mom looked happy to check out the options while we got tacos. Mom rejoined us to enjoy some, too. She had her own new hoard of books.

The owner of the bookstore, and host for the book festival walked around. He saw us and approached. "Looks like you found some new book friends."

Mom nodded. "This is amazing. I love that you do this." She held out her hand. "I'm Rosy, by the way. I'm sure you've met everyone. I just wanted to say, 'Thank You.'"

"Donovan, and it's a pleasure. Take a flier. It gives all the dates for our book events this summer."

"I can't believe you do all of this. I can't imagine. I'm struggling with some idiot who wants to close my bakery back home, and here you are doing this for your community." She breathed deeply. "I wonder if I could do something like this. A street fair to celebrate our town."

"Close your bakery? That's a shame." Donovan shook his head with a sigh. "Just remember, *some* people choose to eat at McDonalds." He waggled his brows, smirked, and headed off to check on some other people.

Not quite getting the joke, I laughed knowing it was supposed to be funny. We checked out the last of the booths we were interested in. Once we'd bought, as Mom put it, a mortgage worth of books.

Charlie licked her fingers. "I know you practically live in a bakery, but isn't there one close to here? I'd love to check out their eclairs, see what they're actually supposed to look and taste like. I want to know if what Pris and I are doing is right."

"I'm also curious if they have any other pâte à choux dough items we could check out." Pris added, her voice becoming very business-like. "I've looked online and have some ideas, but getting the feel and taste makes it easier for me."

Mom's face scrunched up, but finally she nodded. "Right, okay, fine. We can go."

She leaned down and I bumped shoulders with her. "What's wrong?"

"Oh, nothing. I'm just being silly." She shook her head as if to say 'no, forget about it.'

Pris narrowed her eyes. "No, it was something. It's always better to get things off your chest. At least, that's what Dad says, and he's a nurse. He knows how to keep people healthy."

With a sigh, Mom slumped. "The bakery here's one of the Pie In The Sky - Heavenly Delights shops. I'm not exactly thrilled to be supporting them right now. But, that's a 'me' thing. I think the two of you wanting to do a bit of research makes sense, though I do know it's mostly about getting more sugars."

The three of us smiled. Even though we taste-tested all our work in the bakery, any time we could get extra treats was a good day.

We had to drive a few blocks to get to the bakery. Pie In The Sky - Heavenly Delights Bakery had colorful walls, vibrant signs, and the girl behind the counter had a smile that beamed brighter than the lights. I couldn't believe how ... intense it all was. Her eyes widened when she saw us. "Gilly! Is that you? Your hair, what did you do? Are you here with Delia or your mom?"

For a moment I froze, my mind blank, then I shook myself. *Why hadn't I thought of this.* Thank goodness me and the twins had run in ahead of Mom. "Who?"

The worker's eyes widened. "I'm sorry, you look exactly like ... never mind. What can I help you with?"

After doing a circuit of the store, as if casing the place for a remodel, Mom finally made it to the counter. Probably to the worker, Mom looked like she was just interested in what was available for purchase. Finally, Mom searched all the items in the front display counter. "Can we get four Chocolate Eclairs, a dozen Hazelnut spread Profiteroles, a dozen Caramel Profiteroles, a half dozen Choux Puffs, and a half dozen Custard Choux Nuts."

The woman nodded solemnly as she boxed everything together. I felt like my head would explode. Gazing at Charlie and Pris, their eyes looked like they'd pop out of their heads. When the order was done and Mom had paid, we carried it back to the car and Mom put it into the trunk for the drive home.

It took several minutes before I could manage to jump start my thoughts. "I thought you were going to get a couple of things for us to share. I ... um ..." I didn't even know how to ask what I wanted to ask.

Mom's laugh filled the car. "The look on all of your faces made it worth it! I thought we could take it back to the bakery and not only try it all, but try to break down what makes each dessert tick."

"Oh!" Excitement made me dance in my seat. "We can share with Gramps and Cindy."

"That we can. I figure if this is for research, we need to do the work."

From the back, Pris made a small, interesting sound. "If Charlie and I get good at this, could we make a croquembouche for the window?"

Again Mom's enjoyment in the situation filled the car. "We'll see, but there is a good chance. I can't believe you two are taking the bakery in a third direction, but it's exciting, right?"

"It is!" Charlie readily agreed. "I can't believe we won't be able to do any of this baking until next weekend."

"I don't know, we could do some at home after camp. Get some of the mess ups out of the way." Pris chuckled. "Dad loves our kitchen play."

I twisted and leaned back to get closer to them. "We should plan out one or two nights I can sleep over."

I need to help before it's Gilly, not me there to help them.

Charlie already had her phone out. "I'll text Dad, see what he says."

Next to me, Mom shook her head amused at the three of us. I heard her mumble, "The triple terror will take over the world."

Chapter 19 — Take A Number

Rosy

There were several doughs made that I could pull from the fridge. I started there. The display was dangerously low after yesterday ... as were the pre-made stocks.

I can't believe I took most of the weekend off. Despite what the others say, I feel like a truant, and now I'm so behind!

As I got the first batch of Red Velvet into the oven and the next two prepped, I had to admit that I also felt like a fool. Not only had I let myself get drunk, so far gone I couldn't work Saturday, but to what end?

And to top it all off? Elenora Fucking Shifer witnessed it all!

Dad would be here soon to start on his cupcakes. He usually took Tuesdays off. They were a slower day most weeks. He was scheduled to also take off Wednesdays, it was his weekend, but he rarely took off the whole day. Most mornings he showed up to do some baking.

'I'm up anyway, Rosy. What else would I do? Now let me bake!'

When Mom was alive, the two of them used to work as teachers; it's how they met. He taught middle school math and Mom taught high school chemistry. The schools were small and did a lot of crossover in-services.

After they married, it turned out they both loved to experiment in the kitchen, though Dad enjoyed baking more than cooking anything savory. When the school started pushing newer teaching programs every other year and Dad saw I wanted to open this bakery, he decided to jump ship, so to speak, and help me.

I loved watching him manage the girls. They were right in his age range. He always said he chose middle school because those were the kids that needed him the most, for both the math and the social issues. His gruff love really did help a lot of local kids. The parents also loved to come in and kibitz with him.

The bell over the door rang and I heard his heavy tread. He always left the door open behind him. We technically didn't open that early, but it was easier than stopping to officially open the store in about an hour.

I had finished with the Red Velvet and was starting on Bacon Waffle when he made it to the kitchen, quickly taking everything in. "You'll need to make more of that, there isn't enough dough."

"Huh, I would've never considered that. Thanks, Dad." Channeling my daughter, I rolled my eyes and dropped my jaw. I debated putting my hands on my hips, but decided to save that for when the girls were here to rate me.

He came over and kissed my forehead. The side of his mouth quirked up in a smile. "Good to see you back in good form, Rosy."

We spent the next hour mixing ingredients and stocking up on cookies and cupcakes. Something in me settled with the familiar routine. At six-thirty, the first customer walked in.

At the counter stood the man who ran the factory. Like clockwork he showed up every Monday morning. I approached, ready to serve. Curiosity made my smile even bigger than normal as I set to filling his regular order. "What happened with your meeting about no more scented perfumes or lotions?"

He laughed. "For the first two days it got worse." He shook his head. "So much worse. Rosy, you wouldn't believe how bad the place stank. The complaints had never piled up in my office so quickly before. Well, then the person we all thought was the original culprit, and the most frustrated with the rule, Leigh, left on a scheduled vacation. She requested time off a couple of months ago for her daughter's wedding on Saturday in Florida. She left on Thursday. As soon as she left, the issue disappeared."

Once I finished with the box, even before I rang it up, he handed me his credit card. "So, you made the announcement on Monday, the place reeked on Tuesday and Wednesday with a ton of complaints, Leigh leaves Thursday with blissful peace for your nose?"

"Exactly. And the two days it smelled. It was like rank perfume or cologne gone bad. Not even the night cleaners could figure out how, where, or why."

This story had me riveted. "So, what are you going to do next?"

"I had my cousin Stu put some discrete cameras this weekend in a few places where the scent was particularly bad. You know," he started ticking places off on his fingers, "in the hallway by my office, the conference room, the production room, where people clock in. If we can't find the dead skunk," he shrugged, "no idea."

I stacked his order on the counter and he paid. "Good luck."

He made an exasperated face. "Thanks. I hope I have some good news for you next week."

For the next hour, there was a steady stream of people in and out. Tonya came in with her son for her company's regular meeting. Once again, I started on the standing order. "Mom, can I have a cookie that looks like a fudge-filled cup again, oh! They have rainbow cookies, wait, is that an eclair?"

Tonya sighed. "Rosy, one of each, please."

"You always sound so tired. Are things going okay?"

"Yeah, it's just Monday morning." She held up the large coffee that was part of her order. "This always helps." Thankfully she was tired enough not to push me to open a second location. I didn't think I was in the mood for that discussion after the week I'd had.

Things slowed a bit mid-morning, but not much. By nine I was spending about half my time prepping trays and the other half serving customers.

The theater kids came back in. "We need cupcakes," declared their leader, "or the crew will revolt. How can the show go on without cupcakes, fair maid? Tell me thus?"

I laughed as I boxed the choices one of his companions selected. Another two families came in as the group paid in cash, including a lot of coins.

As the next two families decided what they wanted, Dad came up to restock. He looked at the door as another group came in. "This place is a zoo this morning."

"It's been more and more like this lately. That's not a bad thing."

"I know, it's just, wow." He shook his head and headed back to the kitchen.

One of the couples at the counter stepped back, letting the others order ahead of them. *They probably are just trying to decide what sounds good.*

Once the place calmed down, and that couple was the last of the customers, they finally stepped forward. The wife spoke. "Hi, Rosy. I don't know if you know who we are."

I narrowed my eyes and thought. "You're Payge's parents, right? The Whites, Susan and Rick." They always asked me to call them by their first names. When I said their daughter's name, they both winced, and I wasn't sure why. "I used to babysit her when I was a teen."

Susan's nose wrinkled. "Right, it's Weslee now. Or Wes. It has been for a few years. They transitioned right before high school. They approached us ... actually after speaking with your Dad. He never told you about it?"

There was soft chuckling from the back, but I ignored it. "No, Dad never brought work home. And unless Wes had gotten to the point when in Dad's class that—he? they?—wanted others to know, Dad wouldn't have told me."

"Damn right I wouldn't have." His voice wasn't loud enough to carry to the customers, but I heard the pride in it.

"Right, good. That's probably why Wes originally went to him." Susan smiled. "Anyway, Wes has been looking for a job. We think they'd be great here. Not only could they run the counter, they could help with baking as well."

"Um," I said, uncertain what to do. We needed someone, but what if the bakery went under in a month. Could I afford to hire someone? Train someone? Emotions threatened to take me under as I imagined Elenora Fucking Shifer destroying my life's work. I didn't know what to say.

Dad finally stepped out of the kitchen and placed a warm hand on my back between my shoulder blades. "We need the help, Rosy. Why not take Wes on for a two week trial? If it doesn't work out, then we know. But this saves us both from having to do all those things we hate."

A laugh bubbled out of me, and I wondered if anyone else heard the bits of sadness in it. Those things were the steps in finding new employees. Writing an advert, collecting applications, interviewing people, and finding the right fit.

Having a person just fall into our lap, so to speak, was so much better.

"Right, you're all absolutely correct in this. If Wes can show up tomorrow morning, I can start to show um ... them what we do around here. If it doesn't terrify them, we can see what happens next."

Both Wes's parents beamed. Rick nodded. "Excellent. What time should they be here?"

My mouth opened then shut. "I get here at about four, but Dad arrives at four-thirty to five. He probably won't be here tomorrow. So anytime in that window would be great."

He nodded. "I'll let them know."

It surprised me that neither of them seemed to blanch at the early hour.

Late morning was a slow time for us. People finally had their morning fix and were at work. Dad usually had an early lunch while I worked to get more cookies baked.

Based on experience, we'd have another rush around eleven and then, just after twelve it would slow down.

"Rosy, head off to lunch." Dad growled.

"What? I was going to eat here and keep baking today."

"No. Go get Thai. You need something comforting."

I narrowed my eyes at him. "Do you want Thai? Is that it? You're just angling for leftovers?"

His face brightened with a smile. "Go!" He pointed to the door.

The apron caught most of the baking detritus from hours of working, but not all of it. After removing it, I slipped into the bathroom to make sure I wasn't a complete flour monster mess. Then I slipped out to my car to drive the five minutes to Thai Spice. My biggest problem with Thai food was I liked too many dishes. I wanted Pad Thai and Panang Curry and, well, about half the other items on the menu. It was so much better to go with a group and share everything.

When I got to the restaurant, only one of the five tables was still available. I waved at the kitchen staff then pointed at where I wanted to sit. They all nodded at me. I sat, then noticed there was already a menu. *Fuck, this table isn't available.*

Feeling deflated, I was about to get up, when *her* voice washed through me, making my blood sing and boil. *How can one person do so much to me?* "Why hello? Are you crashing my lunch?" *Was that amusement in her voice?*

My muscles tightened, then started to push up.

A warm hand landed on my shoulder, causing tingles of want and need to flood my body. "No, stay. There isn't anywhere else to sit." There was a pause. "Join me, please."

My legs were starting to burn in the half squat position. *God, I need to exercise more.* I closed my eyes and debated running. *That would be childish.* With a big, audible sigh, I nodded. "Okay, fine. But only because I'm starving and their food is beyond words."

I sat back down and faced her, my enemy, Elenora Shifer. She smiled gently. "I was about to order, but, if you're interested, we could combine orders, get more things. I know that sounds forward, but my favorite thing about Asian food is trying ... well, everything."

It was like a punch to the gut. Why did she have to be perfect in every way but one? And that one was so ... big.

"Sure. Sounds great."

One of her brows rose. "What do you like?"

I told her my favorite items. "Oh, love. Let's add Drunken Noodles and an appetizer."

My stomach grumbled its agreement and I nodded. "Okay, but can I put one condition on this meal?"

Her eyes narrowed. "Sure. It isn't that it has to be vegetarian, is it? Because I love beef and shrimp."

"I did say chicken Pad Thai, didn't I?" She visibly relaxed. "But no, I'm open to eating most things." One of her eyebrows shot up, and the side of my mouth twitched. "That said, I was hoping we could not talk shop, if that's okay. Can we limit all conversation to things not bakeries or business related? I don't want my lunch to be stressful."

After a moment of silence where she gazed up at the ceiling as if in thought, her mouth tightening, she finally shrugged. "Okay. I'll meet your conditions, but there are a few things I'd like to iron out with you eventually."

No shit! "I'm sure. Just not at my favorite restaurant. Only good memories here."

It amused me that I was considering a meal with my enemy, even without her bragging about my eventual destruction, a possible good memory, but here we were. *Okay, I'm out to eat with a gorgeous woman. Focus on that. Think about that first night at the bar and pretend you don't know she's evil. Easy.*

A soft smile played across her face. "Okay, we'll go back to when we met. You were Rosy, I was Nora, and we knew nothing else about each other." Her smile grew. "Except you're adorable drunk." Before I could react, she stood. "Speaking of drunk, let me go put our order in."

My mouth gaped open. *She thinks I'm adorable?*

She returned with two Thai coffees. "I wasn't sure if you wanted one of these, but I love them as a treat."

I nearly swooned. Why was she so perfect? "Um, sure. That sounds good. Thanks."

The way her lips wrapped around the straw distracted me and I forgot how to breathe for a few seconds. The server came over and placed plates and glasses of water down. "Not eating alone, this is new. About time." Her voice was sharp and held an edge of finality, breaking me out of my transfixed stare.

"Oh, um, right. We just both needed a table." I answered weakly.

The server's eyes narrowed and she harrumphed before she walked away.

Nora leaned in. "I don't know that she believed you." A sparkle gleamed in her eyes as she reached over and slid a hand in mine. The warmth seemed to infuse into me.

With the feelings I felt, I wasn't sure I believed me either.

She took another distracting sip of her coffee. "So, did you grow up here? Have you always wanted to run a bakery?"

I debated if this came too close to my one condition, but decided this would possibly make me more real. *If I become real to her, maybe she won't want to destroy my world.*

"I did grow up here. My parents were teachers, but both loved being in the kitchen."

"That's how your dad ended up in the bakery with you."

I nodded. "After Mom passed, Dad's heart wasn't in teaching. He retired. Then when I wanted to open the bakery, he joined in." For a moment, I was young again. "He was always the one who baked the sweets whereas Mom did the savory."

Her eyes crinkled at the side with her smile and it made my heart flutter. *Damn it Rosy, this isn't a date.* Despite that her thumb gently rubbed back and forth on my hand and I couldn't ever remember anything being so distracting in my life. *Why is she doing that?*

"My mom was always on a diet. My dad was one of those people who could eat what he wanted and never gain weight. They'd laugh about it." My focus wandered up towards the ceiling. "It's funny. Over the last several years, Dad has put on a few pounds. Not as many as he claims when he says he looks like the cupcakes he bakes, but a few."

Despite myself, as she leaned in while I spoke, I mirrored her action.

Nora's nose scrunched up and I wanted to tap it. *God, I needed to get control over myself. I do not like this person. This was about making me into a person, not her. She is the enemy, evil. Say it again … and again.* Her voice was husky as she asked, "Do you think your mom needed to be on a diet?"

"Maybe. She was hefty but not that big. I think it just stopped her from eating all the sweets in the house. She had a big sweet tooth." I smiled with the memory.

The server came with our food and extra-large plates for each of us. Our hands slowly slid apart, sending shivers up my arm. I rubbed her fingers, as if to prolong the feeling. After shaking my head at my foolishness, I gazed down at the food. "Well, we got the appetizer with everything else. I'm hungry enough to not mind. Shall we dig in?"

"Yes!" Nora said with enthusiasm.

We each started piling food on our plates. It seemed Nora didn't care any more than I did about showing an appetite ... at least not with delicious Thai food.

It only took a few bites, and I moaned with delight, my eyes closing to not let anything distract me from the flavors bursting in my mouth.

Once I'd savored a few bites, I leaned back to sip the Thai coffee. I noticed Nora watching me intently. "What?"

"You're ... I don't know," she shook her head in amusement. "The enjoyment you have in this food ... it's lovely."

"Have you tried it?" I challenged her, narrowing my eyes almost to a Sacia level glare.

"No, I was enjoying the show."

This time I was pretty sure I achieved the full twelve-year-old glare.

As if she recognized it, her eyes widened in mock fear. "Okay, on it."

I watched as she tried everything. This time when her eyes widened, it was with appreciation. After trying each item, I heard soft moans from her as well, and it did something deep within me. Muscles tightened, I feared I may have to find the bedroom toys I had hidden away years ago.

Chapter 20 — The Winners

Gilly

The line in to camp was going so slow today, I could scream. Why couldn't I just jump out here?

"What's the hurry? You'll have all day to be with your new friends." Mom sounded like she was trying to calm a wild beast. *If she only knew how important these few days of summer were to me.*

"I know. I just ..." I wasn't sure how to end the sentence. *After this summer, would I ever see my twin sister again? Would I ever be in this town again?* This was it. A few weeks here and then I'd go back to Milwaukee.

Sure, I could text her and keep in touch on socials, but was that really the same thing?

I should talk with Delia. Maybe she'd have an idea.

The car came to a stop and I scrambled out. "Love you, Mom!" I shut the door on her reply.

"Morning, Sacia!" One of the counselors yelled. I just waved, knowing that would happen with the hair cut. They'd been struggling before, and the only way they knew who was who was because of my longer hair.

Craig is going to flip out. He'll have no way to tell us apart. That thought cheered me up as I ran to the activities field.

As always, I got there before Sacia. My sister. My twin. *My God, I have a twin sister! She has to be my sister.*

Since meeting her, I'd been doing a lot of research on the crash twelve plus years ago ... well, as much as I could. I'd asked Delia to help. She had a friend whose mom had been working at the hospital that night. She had a lot more information.

Apparently, the mom loved seeing Sacia, Charlie, and Pris running around town, knowing the work they did to save the three girls meant that, hopefully, all the kids they saved that night were living happy lives.

The woman confirmed that there had only been one set of twins, and they, along with Sacia and me, were the only kids adopted. All of the other babies had biological families who took them in. It made me happy to know about that.

I wonder if we could find all the kids born that day and have a reunion of sorts. Then again, maybe to some of them it's just a tragic day they lost their parents. Maybe they don't know about a bus full of babies that all survived.

When I got to Craig, as always, he was distracted by whatever he had on his clipboard. I was convinced he hid his phone under some papers and spent his time playing games. I tapped his shoulder. "Morning. Checking in."

His eyes darted up, then back down. "Sacia, you beat Gilly."

"Gilly, and no she didn't."

His face fell and his brows met his hairline. "You got a haircut? How am I supposed to tell you two apart now? This is impossible."

My smile widened. "We always partner up. Just label us, 'The Winners' and assume we're here."

He laughed and I headed off towards the other campers.

It didn't take long for Sacia to join me. She practically tackled me in a hug. "You did it! This is going to be amazing. I can't believe it. My heart is already racing with this idea."

I lightly punched her arm. "It's racing because you ran across the field."

"Well, that too." She smiled. "Okay, so now comes the hard part. We need to tell each other everything about each other's lives, families, homes, how we act. We need to be able to integrate into each other's lives for a full weekend so that the other parent can't tell."

"Should we do it over the weekend or a weekday? You know, like maybe this week we do it Thursday, and next week the weekend. Go more slowly."

Sacia squeezed her eyes shut. "Yeah, I think you're right. But not Thursday, Friday is the Fourth of July, everything is weird. How about Wednesday? Gramps sometimes takes Wednesday off, so he won't be at the bakery when we get there. One fewer person to try to trick."

"Right, Wednesday. That's perfect!"

Chapter 21 — A New Addition

Rosy

The house was dark and still. My alarm would go off in about twenty minutes, but I decided to not try to get more sleep. My mind kept replaying lunch with Nora—Elenora Fucking Shifer—the wicked witch of the east come to town to destroy my business. Despite that, my body buzzed every time I thought of her. *Why do I want to see her again?*

No. I had to focus on my business and family. I had too much to do today.

As quietly as I could, I snuck into Sacia's room and gave her a kiss on the cheek. I couldn't believe how much she'd grown. In a couple of weeks, she and the twins were taking a babysitting training class and then all bets were off. Old enough to be the responsible caregivers in the home.

There were breakfast foods at the bakery. I didn't want to wake either my daughter or Dad, not that he wouldn't be up soon enough., he never slept late. Though Tuesday was technically one of his days off, he sometimes popped in to say 'hi'. Today Weslee worked for the first time. My heart raced both with excitement for the extra help and nerves at knowing I had to train someone alone. I'd woken up early to over prep just in case.

Once at the bakery, I made coffee and a bagel, and then the morning's activities began. As often happened when alone in the bakery, I sank into an almost meditative state—measuring, mixing, chilling, scooping, baking, and decorating. Before I knew it, the front display no longer looked barren and the sun was shining through the front windows.

A knock jarred me from the latest batch of cookies. I shook myself before gazing at my Iwatch. *Six?* "Crap!" I ran to the door to open up. We typically opened earlier, but this was our official opening time. Our first customers had a tendency to arrive a bit later than this.

Standing at the door was a fairly androgynous person in their early mid-twenties with a wide mohawk that was longer in the back. *It's almost like a trendy mullet, if there is such a thing.* They looked stylish, yet not, as if they could care less. They had on a black t-shirt with a stylized pride flag centered over their chest. *Is that asexual or demisexual? Is the frame trans? Gah! I'm going to have to do research ... maybe Sacia knows? Or the twins? Or Dad?*

I realized I'd been studying the outfit too long when I hear Weslee clear her, gah, I'd have to get used to their pronouns ... I was better than this ... their throat. "Sorry, I should've opened the door when I arrived. I got caught up in my baking." I held out my hand. "Weslee, right? It's been so long and you look a bit different."

Weslee chuckled nervously. "Yes! Right in one. And, I don't know if my parents told you, but I use they/them pronouns. If you mess up, it's fine, though I prefer he/him for any mess ups. Also, you can call me Wes ... or Weslee, or you know, whatever. Just not late for dinner." They laughed at their own joke.

"Okay, I can work with that." I stepped back in a half turn, waving my hand out to the side. "Welcome."

They smiled wide. "Thanks." Wes walked in, checking everything out. "I don't know what you were told. I can do anything you want. I'm pretty trainable."

"Sounds good. I figure I'll start by showing you the point of sales. Then, we can move to baking cookies and cupcakes ... though maybe we'll start with just one of them." I bobbed my head back and forth, thinking about the options. "I think two major items is probably more than enough for one day."

Wes gave a shrug. "Up to you."

The first lesson was fast. Wes explained they'd had other customer service jobs and running the till wasn't hard. A few people came in to buy items, and we traded off who took the orders. By eight, it was primarily Wes.

There was a lull at nine, so I pulled them back to the kitchen. "There's usually extra cookie and cupcake batter in the fridge."

As I spoke, they took in both my words and the kitchen. Then they noted, "We're running low on Salted Caramel, and Cookies and Cream cupcakes. So ... more should be made?"

"Exactly." Excitement bubbled in me. Wes was good.

They walked over to the fridge and examined all the labeled bins. After selecting what they wanted, they brought the first batter to the table.

"We usually want to wake it up before using it." I demonstrated what we did, measuring into the pre-lined tins, checking the oven temperature, setting the timer, and inserting the pans.

"Each cupcake has a specific decoration. We have a book here to help us remember what we do." I pulled Dad's cupcake bible from the recipe shelf.

Wes paged through the book. "Oh, this is great if some of the cupcakes aren't in the display. You have the recipes here as well. Maybe if it slows down I could try mixing a batch?"

All the cookies were prepped for the day as well as part of the next. I'd made sure of it that morning. My plan had been to bake brownies that afternoon, though I could hold off on those for a day or two.

"Which cupcake do you want to create?"

They studied the binder. "Could I try the lemon drops? There aren't any out there."

"Sure. Dad hasn't made any in a few weeks. People tend to love them"

"Thanks. I love baking, but my brother ... well, he's diabetic. We try not to have any sugar in the house, or at least not much."

I thought back to when I babysat. Their brother was older than Wes and usually wasn't around when I cared for them. I didn't know much about him. "I'm sorry to hear that. That's rough."

"It is, but he's managing." Wes started poking around the kitchen.

The doorbell dinged. Wes stilled. "I should get that."

"No. You're baking, I'm not. You play with ingredients while I get the town's gossip."

The grin that lit up Wes's face amused me.

I could only see the tops of heads when I came through the door from the back as the customers were bent over looking in the display. When I cleared my throat, both Melody and Latina popped up, smiling at me. "Rosy! Long time and all that." There was a gleam to Melody's eyes.

"It *has* been a couple of weeks. Even longer for you, Latina. How are you two? Is Callen still around?"

They laughed. "That is such old news, you need to catch up with the tea."

As if slapped, I shook my head. "Okay, spill."

Latina crossed her arms on the display. "Okay, you know that our third, Franco, is a photographer, right?"

"I do. He's good. Years ago, when he was starting out, he took some photos for the bakery to help us get up and running, and last fall I saw his stuff at that gallery event. It was stunning."

"Okay, well, a friend of his asked him to be part of their wedding. They've known each other since middle school. Of course, he said yes. Well, this friend *then* asked if Franco would do the photography."

Melody started to laugh and shake her head. "This was so freaking ridiculous!"

I poured them each a coffee, their normal order. As Latina continued her story, Melody pointed to what she wanted.

"Well, Franco emailed his friend saying he'd rather be at the wedding as a guest and not have to work, but if he was their last resort for a photographer, he'd send his normal pricing guide."

That sounded reasonable to me. For a moment my mind imagined my own wedding, but I'd actually have to date for that to ever happen. Nora's image floated through my head … my treacherous mind. *Why her? Why not someone good for me?*

Latina sipped her coffee and sighed. "There was a bit of a delay in the response, but the friend replied, asking if Franco honestly planned to charge that much? Though he didn't want to work the wedding, Franco wanted to be a good friend, so he sent a 'friend's discount' price. He hoped this would finish the discussion. Well, it didn't. His friend was livid that Franco planned to charge anything at all."

This shocked me out of the story and any thoughts of my sexy nemesis. "Wait, what? For real? It's a wedding, there are expenses. In just about any wedding, no matter what, the photographer is one of them. Franco is also a professional, how could they ask someone, even a friend, to do it for free? How much was he charging?"

Melody snickered. I wasn't sure what I said that was so funny, but I figured it was coming out in the story.

"Twenty dollars an hour, all proofs and work included, photos at cost plus ten percent."

I wasn't sure what it all meant, but it sounded better than most deals I'd heard.

"It was at this point Franco debated his decision to even go to the wedding. The three of us, including the new boy, sat down with him to help him brainstorm ways to tell his friend, sorry, but 'no'."

"I was thinking this life long friend was male, is it female? This sounds way more like a bride-zilla thing." I didn't like being sexist, but this was TV-worthy.

Melody held the box of sugars she'd paid for and sat at the one small table we had. She nodded, smiling.

In contrast, Latina shook her head. "Yeah, but not important. Her other friends and family started calling, texting, emailing, and leaving posts to Franco about how they couldn't believe he'd charge the couple. How he was ruining their perfect day. Everything.

"In a fit of frustration, he finally told his friend he'd do it for free, they'd just have to pay for the materials and pictures."

Latina shut her eyes, balled her fists, and took a long calming breath. "Then, this bitch said, 'If you were really my friend, you'd pay me to be my photographer.'"

It was too much. I threw my head back and laughed. Melody laughed with me and in the back, Wes chuckled.

When I got myself under control, Latina stood mute, head shaking. "Two days later we got the invitation for the wedding in the mail. It must have been delayed. Franco could bring one person with him ... his friends all know he's poly. Oh! And all guests are expected to pay one hundred and seventy-five dollars *each* to attend."

My jaw dropped, practically hitting the floor. "Say what?"

"Right? This couple is out of control!"

Melody, eating a cookie from the box, smiled wide. "Isn't it all wacky? Franco spoke to one of the caterers ... also a friend, one who is allowed to charge them apparently. It's costing much less than that per person for the party. They selected a fancy dinner, open bar, elaborate cake, one of those huge ones that has moving parts, but it's still only like a hundred per person, even with the venue."

The story was making my head hurt! "So, not only is this couple not willing to pay Franco, they want all of you to pay, *and* they're trying to make a profit off their wedding?"

"Yep." Latina's voice had an edge to it.

"So, what are you going to do?"

"Franco took a couple of days but finally agreed to his friend's terms." My jaw hit the counter, but both women smirked. "But we're not going."

The laughter echoed throughout the store and kitchen.

Once they left, I went to check on Wes. They were done with the cupcake batter and had filled the first tray. Everything looked great.

I focused on cookies.

When the first batch of lemon drop cupcakes came out, I cut one in half and it looked sellable. For quality reasons, we each ate a half.

The smile on Wes's face was infectious. "I love lemon. Can we make a lemon buttercream to top this instead of vanilla?"

With a bit of work, I blanked my face. Wes looked a bit nervous. My smile broke free, unable to hold the stern expression. "Sure. There should be a recipe near the back. You'll need to do more zesting. Once everything is baked and iced, we'll discuss decorating them."

As the morning progressed, we traded off covering the counter as whoever was best able to leave what we were doing. It felt as comfortable as when Dad was in the kitchen with me. It pleased me at how well Wes seemed to fit in with me and how the bakery ran.

The warmth slipped away as a cold dread washed through me. *What if everything crumbles to the ground because of that Shifer woman and her plans to take over my town? Have I just given Wes hope of a job only to dash it away?*

Just after eleven, the bell rang. Wes had a piping bag in their hands and buttercream ... everywhere. Biting my bottom lip, I said, "Got it."

Once I could see the door, I smiled at who arrived. Cindy approached with a shit-eating grin on her face. "Hiya Rosy, how are you doing today?"

"Hey! I'm supposed to be the greeter here, it's my bakery." I waggled my brows. "And, I'm doing great." I leaned my head back a bit and called, "Wes, come meet my best friend, she'll be here a lot so you should know her."

Wes came out and was still covered with lemon-scented buttercream. Cindy's eyes widened. "Are you practicing on yourself before the cupcakes? Because it's not easier, you know."

Wes blushed. "It's my first day." They looked down. "And this way I have some for later."

Cindy slapped the counter and busted out laughing. "Oh, I like this one." She narrowed her eyes on Wes's shirt. "Okay, I know the flags on the shirt. What are your pronouns?"

Eyes wide, Wes beamed. "They/them. Thanks." After that, they spun and headed back into the kitchen.

I just stared at Cindy. "What did I miss?"

"Knowing you? Everything. Living in this building means you know pretty much nothing of the greater world. I spend my time in a library and get more exposure to things."

We both reacted when we heard the water running in the kitchen. Wes had been here about five hours. "Wes, have you had a break? If not, take one."

"Okay."

"Already working the new staff to the bone?" One of Cindy's eyebrows rose.

"Of course. Now it's been weeks, are there cat updates? I can't believe you haven't told me anything about Sir Fluffy Butt." I poured two coffees and handed one to my friend.

She sighed as she took hers. "God, that animal. Selena suggested I get the damn thing a collar since it likes to go outside. She's afraid it'll go out some day and never return."

"Has it ever been gone for an extended amount of time?"

"It's usually home by supper. The animal loves to eat." Cindy pointed to a Peanut Butter cookie. I handed it to her. Defiantly, she dropped some money on the counter. We'd been fighting over her paying for years. She helped out in the bakery and with Sacia, but I feared I wouldn't win this one.

With a sigh I rang up the order and gave her the change.

"So, what are you going to do? Has any name won out for the mangy mongrel?"

"Well, I call the cat Idiot a lot, and Fuzzy Butt, and tell the beast he's lucky he's cute ... because he is."

"But no official name yet?"

"Nope, I'm debating just naming him Fred or Doe, or Joe Blow." Cindy shrugged.

"Or," I lifted my hands towards her, palm out, as if giving her this Earth shattering idea. "Crazy thought here. You could finally just fess up to Selena."

Before Cindy could respond, Wes came out holding a Peanut Butter cookie of their own. "You know, this cookie would go great with ice cream."

"Yeah." I smiled as Cindy smirked. *What is she thinking?* "I've had that thought in the past. Maybe we could add another part to the bakery in the future."

Wes nodded excitedly while Cindy's face scrunched into confusion. She tilted her head. "So, tell me about lunch yesterday."

I felt like I'd get whiplash with the change in subject. "What? Where did that come from? Lunch?"

"Just curious."

"I went to Thai Spice, it was great." *Mostly.*

Her eyes narrowed. "So, a quiet meal alone?"

I slumped. "Well, no. The evil queen of," rolling my back towards Wes, I shrugged, "well, you know. Let's just say I had an unexpected companion. We didn't talk shop, as per my meal guidelines ... I wanted a pleasant meal. In the end, well, it was fine, I guess."

Again, Cindy's face scrunched up. "Got it. Well, I'm here for the next hour. Go, eat. I can be here for a couple of hours tomorrow, so you can take a longer break, especially with Wes here. I'll get to know them better. I think the two of us will become fast friends."

It felt like Cindy had something more to say, but I wasn't sure what. But, I was hungry and wanted lunch. "I'll be back in an hour. I'm heading home today to eat with Dad."

"Good. But tomorrow go somewhere good so you can bring me something back for my lunch." She winked.

"Fine, whatever. Love ya!"

"Love you, too, Rosy, now go!"

I explained the afternoon to Wes and headed out. I had a nagging feeling Cindy wasn't telling me something, but for the life of me, I wasn't sure what it could be.

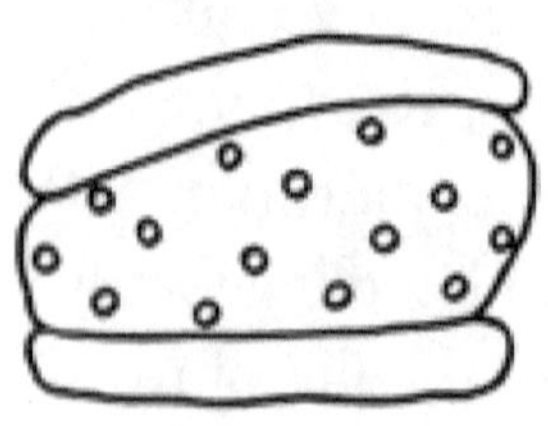

Chapter 22 — Business Before Pleasure

Nora

Sitting outside the ice cream factory, I waited for Fe. We had a meeting with the Hernandez family at nine.

This is it. If I can convince them of my vision, then I won't only grow my business, I can diversify. And then not only will I have a bigger portfolio, maybe the alluring Rosy won't hate me. Stop it! I have to focus! No distractions before a big meeting.

At a quarter to nine, Fe drove into the parking lot. We both got out of our cars. Fe smiled. "Are you ready?"

"I am. Not only have I looked over the reports you sent, I did some comparative analysis of desserts and sales in different towns throughout small towns in Wisconsin, Michigan, Illinois, and Minnesota. I want to show them that what we're proposing will help both our brands."

My assistant smiled. "Sounds like you've done a lot of prep, boss."

"If I'm right, and this flourishes, we can continue to build store fronts more easily than the regular bakeries. Product is sent to the ice cream stores, not baked on site. This could take the brand to a new level." A giddiness filled me.

Fe smiled wide. "Let's get in there and kill it!"

The meeting took a couple of hours. Instead of meeting with just Mrs. Hernandez, we met with the family. Once done, Fe and I drove to a park down the road with a shelter and tables. The day was too nice to not enjoy.

As always, Fe had out a pad of paper and a grin ... today's was shit eating. "You did great, boss, I love seeing you in action."

"Thanks, for a few minutes I didn't think we'd make it past Mrs. Hernandez's arsenal. Her husband enjoyed the show, but that woman is fierce."

Fe nodded. "Okay, I have all their signed Non-Disclosure Agreement, so I know they won't try to take our plans to someone else. They seem like an above board family, but we have to be careful. I also have the changes the middle son, Alejandro, and Mrs. Hernandez both demanded. I think the others were there as a show of force."

From our years together, fighting for my other shops, I knew Fe was correct. "Okay, get the new contract written and get a meeting with the two of them for next week. We can read over the contract once you're done. We need to make sure we have a lock on the old doll-store. Maybe contract a wiccan to do a full seance, sage-burning, the works. I don't know if I want the old mojo lingering."

Fe snorted. "Do you want me to look into that, or is that on your list?"

"I'll take that one."

"Great. Then let me know if there's anything else we need to do on this one."

My smile hurt my cheeks. "Perfect. Thank you again."

Back in my car, I let out a relieved, "Yes!" I tried to be confident from the moment I walked into the factory, but there had been some time at the start I wasn't sure.

I leaned my head back and finally relaxed, then pulled my phone out and turned it on.

In reality, I didn't think there would be an issue with Gilly and the camp had Delia's number, but if anyone had needed me, it would've been when I was unavailable.

I did have a text, but it wasn't from Delia or the camp, it was from Cindy. *What could she want?*

'Hi, I know we just met, but, did you tell Rosy about your new business plan?'

How could I explain? Maybe she knew how her friend was. *'I didn't. Rosy made me promise to keep business out of the meal.'*

The indication of Cindy's reply popped up right away, surprising me. *'She's having lunch at the Burger Shack. You should go and tell her. Today.'*

My mind drifted to Rosy and her luscious curves. I let myself moan in appreciation of her beauty. There weren't any witnesses this time. "God, what am I going to do?"

Chapter 23 — A Burger With A Side Of Lies?

Rosy

Even though I spent most of my day on my feet, I decided to walk to lunch. The Burger Shack was two blocks from the bakery. It was a beautiful day and the sun and cool breeze soothed my soul.

I felt a bit guilty getting burgers without Sacia; I knew she and the twins loved this restaurant, but I needed something close and satisfying. For the girls, it wasn't the food as much as the atmosphere. The wait staff dressed as if they were from the fifties, they called everyone 'sugar' or 'love', and there were games for the kids to play. The fact that the food tasted great was just a bonus.

When the girls were helping out, Cindy brought them here often.

Being summer, there was a wait to get a table. The front was full of people sitting and standing, kids jabbering, playing on their phones, and noise. So much noise.

The host said, "Don't worry, Cookie-Slinger. We'll get you a table in a jiffy. You'll be back to creating more magically delicious baked goods for the town in three shakes of a heifer's tail." He handed me the disc-shaped pager.

As I turned to find a place to sit and wait, I nearly ran into Nora, who held a flashing and beeping disc. *God she's scrumptious ... or am I just really hungry. God, her table's ready, apparently. Well, I can take the place she'd been sitting.* Except a young couple swooped in and took the seats.

Nora smiled sheepishly. "We seem to be having similar lunch thoughts. Would you care to join me, again? I seem to have a table and I'm guessing there is more than one seat."

"Sure, but only if—"

"Follow me, love, or we'll move on to the next." An older woman rolled up in skates, a poodle skirt, and a button down tied at her waist. *How does she not run into everything?*

Before I could figure out what was happening, Nora linked her arm in mine and led me with her as we tried to follow the host as she twirled and sped through the crowd.

Nora's lips brushed near my ear, and shivers played throughout my body. "I have no idea how she does that. I feel like I'm going to fall just watching her."

A manic laugh burst out of me and I slapped my free hand over my mouth. That was too close to what I'd been thinking, and there were too many sensations. I couldn't sort them all out. Thankfully, we were led to one of the tables just big enough for two at the side of the restaurant, away from most of the hustle and bustle of the other diners. The host eyed me for a moment, then grinned. "I'll take your name off the list, Cookie Goddess, if you'll give me your beeper."

In a daze, I did as she asked. Nora pulled out my seat, securing me in place, before sitting herself.

The action felt awkward and charming all at the same time. "Tell me, what's good here?"

I closed my eyes and shook my head, taking a moment to center myself. The absurdity of everything washed through me and I smiled. "Mostly everything. I usually get the Shake Burger with jalapeno medallions, chipotle aioli, bacon, cheese, and, you know, the works. When I'm feeling saucy or daring, I'll upgrade the fries to onion rings."

"So, they make good onion rings? I know they can be hit or miss at different establishments. What about the tater tots?"

I groaned. "The best, especially the loaded tots. Usually I'm here with a gaggle of ... well, I'm not usually here alone."

One of her brows rose. "More stories?"

"Maybe, maybe not." I leaned back and narrowed my eyes debating if I should tell her about Sacia. And if I did, should I tell her the full story or just that I had a daughter. *Are we ready for personal stories?* "I just can't figure you out."

"Me? I'm easy. I'm a woman, looking at one of the sexiest ladies I've ever seen, trying to explain to her that an ice cream shop isn't any competition to her bakery, but she won't listen."

Everything in me stilled and I gaped at her, not sure if I heard her right or even believed her. Was she lying?

"What'll you have?" The server asked.

Unable to wrench my gaze from Nora, I tried to say something but couldn't get it out. Nora took over, ordering burgers for both of us, and loaded tots and onion rings for the table.

The server winked. "Sounds great, my lovelies. And to drink?"

Nora's eyes narrowed, then she gave me a wicked grin. "Two chocolate shakes."

Out of the corner of my eye, I saw the server smile, take the menus, and head off. Then, Nora reached across the table and slid her warm hands under mine. "You okay? Still with me?"

Again, I needed to block out all the extra stimulations. I closed my eyes, but squeezed her hands to let her know I was okay. "An ice cream shop?"

Can it be the truth? Is it possible her goal isn't to destroy my bakery? My mind couldn't decide if

I believed her or just *wanted* to believe her. *Can I surrender to all these feelings?*

"Rosy, look at me."

I took one more deep breath, smelling all the grease and hamburgers, trying to tune out the laughter and talk from around us. There were families and kids, sounds from games, and squeals of what I hoped was delight. Moreover, my body vibrated from the contact between us, something that had been happening since we'd met in the bar on my birthday.

One more breath and I opened my eyes. My full vision was taken up by the light green of Nora's eyes and her slight smirk. "There you are, beautiful." She squeezed my hands. "When I first wanted to expand, the idea was another bakery, but when we settled on Pekara, we saw there already was a thriving bakery. We knew one of two things would happen. Either we'd be great at the expense of another small business—something I never wanted—or we'd fail. That last was not an option." She bit her lower lip. "And then there's this town. It's lovely ... and you ... um, well, the town, it loves you." she shook her head and smiled.

My eyes misted as I heard the sincerity of her words. For a moment if felt like she was going to say something else, but I must've imagined it. "Why didn't you tell me?"

She laughed, and I wanted to drown in that sound. I could imagine it mixed with the laughs of the other people in my life. It would fit in so well with the symphony I could hear in my mind.

God, what am I thinking? She's here for a few weeks. Even if it isn't a bakery, she lives in Milwaukee, not here. It isn't like this thing will be long term. Get it together, Rosy. Just because she thinks you're pretty, don't fall for the first person you've had a meal with in ... gah! In several years.

Nora's eyes narrowed. "What happened? You were smiling, and then your face fell." Her head tilted. "No, let me start by answering your question. I've been trying to tell you for days. When we first met ... Well, at the bar on your birthday we didn't know each other, but the day at the bakery, you just kicked me out. Then yesterday, you told me we weren't allowed to talk shop."

"But I made that condition today, as well." I reminded her.

"No." Her face beamed. "You started to, but were interrupted. I wasn't sure how I would get out of it, but I knew I had to get the information out fast … in case you remembered."

Thinking back, I realized she was right. I started to demand 'no work,' but hadn't secured the agreement. *Me and my brilliant ideas.* "So, you're going to compete with Screaming Fun Ice Cream and the Hernandez's? Do you know what you're getting yourself into?"

She snorted. "I wouldn't pit my worst enemy against Mrs. Hernandez. She's a beast. But no, I'm not competing with them, I'm working with them. A partnership. I want to sell their ice cream and fix the shop at their factory so that they actually have a shop."

My mouth dropped. "About freaking time." My heart beat faster. "This town will be a hotspot. This sounds amazing. Though, I still worry about my bakery. The ice cream shop is the better investment."

"Not when the biggest item is cookies and cream with your cookies, or ice cream sandwiches, or any number of collaborations between the stores. I want Pekara to be the sugar capital of Wisconsin."

Chills raced up and down my spine as the server brought us our drinks. "You're serious, aren't you?"

"I'm always serious when I'm talking business ... or trying to woo an alluring woman. Combine the two and all bets are off."

My mouth was suddenly dry and I had no idea what to say. Trembling, I reached for my chocolate shake and took a long sip. I almost gave myself brain freeze.

Nora's eyes bore into me. "Okay, out with it. You keep disappearing into yourself."

I forced myself back into the conversation. "Sorry, it's all just so overwhelming. I never imagined that you'd do anything like this." *Can I really have my cake and eat it too?* I almost snorted.

We spent the rest of the meal enjoying our food and discussing why she'd decided to shift from a bakery to ice cream.

We didn't have a ton of time since I had to get back to work. Outside the Burger Shack, I turned towards Main Street.

"Wait, Rosy, I'd really like to have a meal with you that we plan out, not just a chance meeting."

All my muscles tensed and I gazed into her face, her eyes becoming ... everything. *A date? I can date Elenora Shifer? What has happened to my world?*

A decision had to be made. On the one hand, I could have fun while she was in town. On the other, I faced potential heartbreak. *Get over yourself, just have some fun. Remember what it's like to date. You can find your 'forever person' once you relearn how to date.* Finally, smiling, I nodded. "Okay, yes, I think I'd like that, too."

"Wow, you sound so into this." One of her brows shot up.

My shoulders dropped. "Sorry. I haven't done anything like this in ... well, in a while. We can hold that story off for the third date."

Nora beamed. "Well now, if we count the lunches, won't the next one be the third?"

I laughed, releasing a bit of my tension. "Maybe. If you're lucky."

She leaned towards me. "I hear the third date *is* the lucky one." My blush burned my cheeks and Nora reached out to cup my face. "I like you, Rosy Roads. I look forward to our next rendezvous."

She stepped close and slowly bent down until we met in a kiss. My lips parted and she deepened the kiss. The world receded and I reached out to hold her slender hips, lest I fall. Heat and passion swelled in me, threatening to drown me, until all I knew was Elenora Shifer.

Chapter 24 — It's All In The Details

Gilly

Charlie grabbed my arm as I finished my last event in the full camp scavenger hunt and dragged me towards the bathroom. They seemed to have some sort of full camp competition every other day. It probably wasn't that often, but it was a way to keep us all busy, force us to partner with different people, and allow the counselors some down time.

It seemed to me like Sacia and the twins knew where everything was and about everything. No matter who they partnered with, the three of them were in the top three finishers. They didn't compete with the other campers, they competed with each other. I had a feeling that was how they were in school as well. It was a hoot watching them and hanging out with them.

Hoot? Darn it! Mom's weird words are following me around!

"What are we doing here? I don't need to go, you know." I laughed as she dragged me into the stinky place I usually avoided. I could hear other voices within.

She abruptly stopped at the restroom door, knocked in an odd pattern, and turned to me with a smile. "You're just like your sister, brilliant to a fault, the fault being the details."

Sister! God, she just said that! My heart beat faster and I started to dance in place, like I always did right before a track meet. The words thrilled me—*Just like your sister.* "Okay, genius friend of mine, what am I missing?"

The door opened and Pris grabbed my hand, yanking me forward. "You can't go home with Rosy dressed like that, silly. Even if she weren't there when Sacia left for camp, she'd know those weren't clothes she bought or ever washed."

I banged my head with the heel of my hand. *Why hadn't I thought of that?* Sacia wasn't immediately visible, but one of the bathroom stall doors was closed. Her voice came from the other side. "Toss me your clothes over the wall, mine are draped to the left, wait, my left, your right."

My hands shot up making two L's, my trick to tell my left from my right. I went into the stall on the side of the backwards L. As we changed, they went over the details one more time. I echoed what Sacia would need to know.

Charlie said, "Sacia always sits in the front seat, seatbelt on, bag by her feet, but twists to be able to talk with us."

"I sit in the front as well, bag at my feet. Only difference is, no one in the back seat."

Pris spoke next. "I asked my parents if we could hang out at our house this afternoon. We'll start at the bakery, so you can see it, but we'll walk to our house after about a half hour. That way we should be able to avoid any baking."

I let out a sigh of relief. That had been the one real issue. The other three baked all the time, and I had no idea what to do in the kitchen. The twins said they'd figure it out and all I could do was trust them. "Thank you, that sounds perfect."

"Of course," Pris sounded excited. "Then you get to see our place as well. Someone will come around to pick you up so that you can head home ... well, to Sacia's home for dinner."

Excitement prickled my arms and belly. This was all actually happening. I was going to see how my sister lived. I didn't know why this was so important to me, but it was. We were both adopted. But for some reason, I—we—both wanted to experience each other's lives. It would give us a feel of what we both had growing up. Let us get a bit closer to each other.

I stepped from the stall and saw Sacia standing there in my clothes. Even more than the first day I saw her, it felt like I looked in a mirror. For a moment my mind whirled, then I smiled and tackled her in a hug. *This is really going to happen!*

Sacia held back. In the two weeks of camp, her mom was always second to drop off and first to pick up. We watched the line, just in case, and saw the cars. She knew which car was mine, and sure enough, her mom was almost at pick up when I saw Mom's car pull into the lot. "Okay, there she is." I gave Sacia one more hug. "You'll be great!"

"Have fun, Gilly." She hesitated. "Love you!"

I had to blink back tears. "Love you too!"

With my heart in my throat, I ran with Charlie and Pris to meet Ms Roads. They waved me to the front. *It's just my mom's car. It's just my mom's car.* It was so much more awkward than I thought. Swallowing back all my fear, I leapt in, as if Mom sat next to me, dropped my bag, as if I did this every day, buckled in—*oh yeah, this is normal*—and twisted to look at first Ms Roads ... no, Mom, and then the twins.

"How was camp today? Was there a scavenger hunt that the three of you dominated, as always?" Ms Road's warm smile filled the car. She had brown wavy hair that dipped past her shoulders and gray eyes that I feared saw past my disguise. *Does she know? Could she suspect?*

Don't be silly, how could she?

"No," I shook my head. "I mean, of course. The counselors make the clues too easy."

Charlie snorted. "They should let Pris make the challenge and we could send the counselors on it. Then *we* could sit back playing on our phones."

We all laughed.

I wanted to say ... something. I had no idea what to say to this stranger. The back of my mind screamed to say anything. *What would I say to Mom?* In desperation, I looked back at my friends, they circled their hands, as if to say, go on, say something. I sneered, no help there.

"How was your day?"

Ms Roads shot me a look, one brow raised. *Maybe Sacia never asked that.* "Good. Wes is doing great. If this continues, I may be able to adjust my hours, have more time away from the bakery. Maybe we can do more adventures like the one we did on Sunday."

Sunday? Oh, they went to that book festival! They met the authors.

"That would be amazing. I'll just need to find more authors to meet. I'm sure I can do that."

Ms Roads laughed. "I'm sure you can. Just keep it within a few hours drive. No book festivals three states away, okay?"

I scrunched up my face and bobbed my head back and forth in thought. "I'll consider it."

"I'm sure you will." Her head tilted up. "I hear you're all abandoning me to my own baking devices today. No eclairs today?"

Charlie sighed. "No, we'll be back at it tomorrow. Personally, I like having Gramps there to grumble at us as we make the pâte à choux."

"Same." Pris agreed. "I think it adds just the right amount of spice to the recipe."

Laughter filled the car. Sacia's mom navigated through traffic as she said, "That tracks, I'm guessing that's what makes Dad's cupcakes as good as they are. He claims it's because he looks like one, but I'm guessing it's his snarling."

I chuckled as Ms Roads finally parked. Everyone in this family were dorks, and I loved it.

We piled out and headed into the bakery. I'd been in and out of bakeries my whole life, but this one had a homey feel. I instantly loved it. Ms Roads was ahead of me, so I took a moment to gaze around, looking at everything.

The woman behind the counter snorted. "See something new, Sacia, or are you planning a remodel, finally?"

Behind me, Pris said, "Afternoon, Cindy, has the place been busy?"

I narrowed in on Cindy. This was one of the important people they spoke of a lot. Ms Roads's best friend and a person who not only watched after them but took them places. She had short curly black hair, but only on the top, as if she didn't want to bother with longer hair. She had dark brown eyes and a wide smile.

"Okay you three, I know you're only here for a bit, but come back and help with a few things." Ms Roads's voice floated from the back of the store.

My heart dropped.

Cindy's eyes narrowed. "What's wrong, kiddo? You look like you saw a ghost, or maybe a ghost pepper."

Pris linked her arm in mine. "She's fine. Long day at camp, that's all."

The back kitchen was huge. Bigger than I'd imagined it would be. *How could it fit within the confines of this building? Is this building a TARDIS?* I huffed out a small laugh at the thought. *I wonder if any of my new friends like that show, or fantasy, or ... focus Gilly!*

"I know you're leaving soon so you can meet your Dad, but I have a few things that won't take more than a minute. Okay Charlie, Wes has mixed up a new batch of Salted Caramel cupcake batter. Can you get the extra stored away? Pris, same with my extra Red Velvet cookie batter. That way we can work on decorating. Sacia, I have three pans of brownies that just need slicing." She smiled at us. "See, none of that should take long or be hard."

I started to tremble, but, I could cut brownies. I'd done that before.

I walked over to the pan and gazed at the delicious looking and smelling dessert. Thankfully, there was a knife right there. I picked it up, feeling it for its heft. *Okay, I can do this, it's just cutting brownies. I think I can, I think I can, I think I can.*

As I gazed down at the dessert, it occurred to me I didn't know how many slices, but if I asked, it would give away too much. I stood frozen, knife in hand, unsure what to do.

I remembered brownies Mom had made for a track meet. They'd been so good. She'd ended up baking three trays. I think each tray was about this size. Did she cut them into nine pieces? Sixteen? Twenty-five? Were they square?

A hand landed on my shoulder and I nearly jumped. "Sacia!" My head snapped around and another hand wrapped around my wrist. "Whoa there slasher. Are you okay? I called your name a few times and you didn't respond. And then there's the fact you're holding the knife in your, as you've often put it, useless left hand."

All my muscles tensed. *How could I forget that Sacia used her right hand?* "I um ..." I had no idea what to say.

"Let me explain ..."

"She's fine ..."

Both Pris and Charlie started to talk.

One stare from Ms Roads stopped them both. "Something's going on here." Her hand slid up to mine, and she worked the knife away from me. Her eyes narrowed and a small smile played across her face. "Okay, who are you and what did you do with my daughter?"

It felt like I'd been electrocuted as shock spread out throughout my body.

Behind Ms Roads, the twins started talking again. I couldn't make out their words, but apparently Ms Roads could. Her eyes widened and she stepped away from me swinging her gaze back and forth, taking us all in. "Stop. I was only kidding. You're telling me that this isn't Sacia Roads, my daughter?"

Chapter 25 — We'll Have Two Of Everything

Nora

Every movement Gilly made since leaving camp had been more hesitant than normal. It wasn't that she was acting differently, just less. *Maybe she's sick. She usually doesn't get sick, but she is outside with a bunch of kids all day, that usually is a recipe for disaster.*

"I'm ... if it's okay, I'm going to go to my room for a few minutes."

When was the last time she asked? "Dinner will be ready in about an hour."

"Oh! Do you want hel—I mean, what are you making?"

I squeezed my eyes shut. This had to be my mind playing tricks. Gillyflower Shifer did not just almost offer to help in the kitchen. The girl was allergic to the room. There was no way. I was definitely imagining things.

God, I hope this whole day hadn't been a dream, I enjoyed lunch way too much.

"I was thinking spaghetti with meatballs, something simple."

She smiled. "Sounds great."

Before she could leave, my phone rang. It was Rosy. I was both confused and surprised at seeing her number. "Rosy?"

Halfway down the hall, I saw Gilly stop and look back, her eyes wide. *Does she know the bakery owner? Has Rosy catered at the camp?*

Rosy had been speaking and I had to playback in my mind what she'd said. "Dinner? Tonight? I know I mentioned going out again, but I'm not good with short notice."

"I get that, but there's something um ... incredibly important I need to show you." *Does she sound distracted? Nervous? Angry?*

"Can it wait? I ..." I'd avoided bringing up Gilly, it seemed a bit personal, but she was the reason I couldn't go out. "Look, I have a daughter. I can't just leave her."

"I ... bring her." Did she sound excited? Eager? "We can go to this great cajun restaurant on the other side of town. They make the best gumbo."

"Gumbo? Cajun?" I couldn't imagine having good gumbo in Pekara, Wisconsin. Not to mention, Gilly eating it.

"I'm sure your—daughter—would enjoy it."

I scoffed. "I doubt Gilly would try gumb—"

"I would. It sounds ... um, fun!" She interrupted, perking up at the last word, as if truly excited for gumbo. I narrowed my eyes, wondering what had happened to my daughter since I'd dropped her off at camp that morning.

On the way over to the restaurant, Gilly received a few texts, but when I asked her, she shrugged saying it was one of her friends from camp reminding her about Friday.

"Since Friday is the fourth of July, tomorrow is like Friday, so we don't do the normal activities."

"Ah, so no track and field?"

Her face scrunched up. "Pretty much."

I reached over and ruffled her hair. "I know, you love getting out there to run. Maybe we can head back to Milwaukee this weekend and you can get out to the track. Unless you have a better idea."

She mumbled something, but I didn't quite hear it. "What was that?"

"Nothing, sorry."

"No, tell me. We don't keep secrets, you know that." *At least I hope we don't.*

A look crossed her face for a moment as if my words hurt her, then she sighed. "I have some friends in town. I thought maybe we could do something like the ice cream factory tour. You know, something in town."

What is going on with this girl? "You want to do the tour again? Do you think you'll learn something new?"

She gasped and shook her head. "I mean, no. Something *like* that tour." Her face reddened and she began to squirm.

"You okay?"

She pointed. "Look, there's the restaurant."

I pulled into the parking lot and figured she and I could have a heart to heart after dinner. Maybe she was as hungry as me, and that was why she was acting so weird. If not, we needed to have a discussion ... soon.

"Table for two? Oh! No, you're with Rosy, right?"

Next to me, Gilly had a wide grin on her face. Again, I wondered what was up with her. "Yes." The host led us to a table. There were four place settings and I sat next to Rosy, letting Gilly sit across from someone she didn't know.

Before she sat, she looked at each of us. "I'm sorry, the restroom ... it's an emergency. If the server comes, just order me whatever. I'm sure you know what I like." Her smile got bigger and bigger as she spoke, then she darted off.

My mouth hung open and my hand waved in the direction of my disappearing daughter. "Well, meet my daughter ..." Rosy watched her run off, a small smile on her face as I spoke.

"Hi! I'm Gilly! Nice to meet you." Gilly plopped down in the chair next to me. "Hiya mom." She smiled and it seemed so much more relaxed than it had been all afternoon.

"I thought you were heading to the bathroom."

"Ma'oom! You know me, I'm fast!"

A laugh bubbled out of me. It was the first genuine thing I'd heard from this girl all afternoon and muscles that had been tense began to relax. "Okay, let's check out this menu. Figure out what you should eat."

"Oh, um, gumbo, like Rosy said, that sounded great. You know, I see someone from camp, I'll be right back." She darted away before I could say yes or no, or even ask what proteins she wanted.

Rosy chuckled next to me. "She's a delight." My head swung from my darting daughter to the beauty next to me. About to respond ...

"Thank you!" Gilly said, sliding back into the seat.

On my other side, Rosy's eyes narrowed. "What kind of gumbo do you want ... Gilly?"

Was there an odd pause to her question? Is everyone messing with me?

Gilly shrugged, then opened the menu ... finally. "I think sausage and shrimp sounds good."

The server arrived and we ordered. Rosy asked for a second gumbo and jambalaya. Personally, I thought the shrimp po-boy sandwich sounded good.

Once everything was ordered, Gilly looked at us, then asked, "There were some pictures by the entrance of New Orleans, do you think I could go check them out while we wait for the food?"

"Sure, but don't take too long." I watched her run off towards the front door, then turned to smile at Rosy, trying to relax and enjoy myself. "How was your day?"

"Mine was great!" Gilly plopped down, approaching from behind. "Camp was a lot, but soon it'll be the weekend. I'm super excited. I think we should go to the chocolate factory, do that tour next."

And my relaxation was gone. My head was going to explode. Like brain matter everywhere. "So, you've decided. Just like that. In the car nothing, but now?"

The server came with drinks and a tray with crab cakes and hush puppies. I gazed at the food. "I don't think we ordered this."

Rosy smiled up at the server. "Thank you." She smiled sheepishly at me. "I ordered this before you got here. I wasn't sure how well you knew the food and I ordered—"

Gilly flew to the table and sat. "You got appetizers! Thank you, thank you, thank you!"

No wait, Gilly was already at the table, she couldn't have ran and sat down across from me at the empty seat. She couldn't be serving a plate of food to herself ... and herself.

A warm hand rubbed my arm. "Just breathe. This is why I insisted we meet tonight."

It took a huge act of will to tear my eyes from the mirror image girls and face Rosy. "What's going on?"

"From what I understand, both Sacia and Gilly were adopted from the bus crash twelve years ago."

For a moment, my fight or flight kicked in, but then my brain caught up and realized she wasn't saying anything I couldn't figure out. She wasn't trying to take my child. Gilly was my daughter and would stay that way. "Okay. Go on."

She reached over and grabbed a crab cake and took a bite. "After I brought Sacia home, I met another family in town who had adopted from the crash. We ended up raising the kids together, partially to help each other out, they work odd hours, and so do I."

"That sounds ... nice for the kids." I had no idea where she was going with this.

"The other family ended up with twins, but they weren't identical. If I were to make a guess, the hospital made a mistake since there was so much trauma and confusion that night. I believe our daughters are the real twins."

Both girls squealed and hugged each other, then separated, wiggling in their seats exactly alike. It occurred to me they were the same in every way ... except their shirts. "For fuck's sake!"

"Mom! Language."

I snorted. "Sorry. It's just that the two of you aren't wearing the same shirt, and I didn't even notice until now."

Rosy laughed. "I was wondering if you'd figure that out sooner. The speed at which they were moving, it wasn't easy."

"Wait, how did you figure it out?"

Across from me, not-Gilly—*did she say Sacia?*— Glared between her mom and Gilly. "Yeah, I was doing great, what gives?"

"Eh." I held out my hand and wiggled it back and forth. "I'd give you a C minus."

Gilly hugged her stomach laughing as Rosy told her story.

Chapter 26 — Sugar Buns

Rosy

My body buzzed as I filled the display with the remaining Italian Rainbow cookies. *Sacia will need to make more, we're almost out of her specialty. Good thing the camp is closed tomorrow and I can drag her in to do her unpaid job.*

I paused and thought about her spending the night with Gilly last night. The two girls had been over the moon at dinner and once Nora calmed down, dinner had been great.

Once Nora calmed down ... have I calmed down? Have I mentally figured this all out? My God, Sacia has a twin sister, and it's Elenora Shifer's daughter. What is this world coming to?

Stepping back from the display, I shook out my hands to release the tension that suddenly infused me. It had been coming in waves ever since I'd learned about this. I didn't know what to do, the girls had instantly clicked, and Pekara to Milwaukee wasn't *that* far away, but I was guessing, for them, it was too far. They were literally like two peas in a pod.

If I could go back and strangle those hospital staff ... I wouldn't. They had been swamped with a busload of heartache and trauma. The fact that they'd saved all the babies had been amazing. I won't begrudge them a thing. Especially the fact that I ended up with Sacia, my wonderful daughter, but the girls missed out on twelve years together.

The bell chimed and I shook myself from my thoughts. Looking up, I saw Wes walk in. "Morning boss!"

The side of my mouth twitched. "Morning."

It didn't take more than a few seconds for them to figure out what was going on. "I'll finish up the display, I'm sure there's some cookies that need to be baked. Once I have everything filled, wiped down and cleaned, and the coffee prepped for customers, I'll swing back for my orders."

"Coffee, that sounds perfect. Thank you."

"It's my job." They winked and I headed to the back. I had prepared the first batch of Crumble S'more, a popular cookie, especially this time of year, when Wes placed a coffee next to me.

"Thank you! I need more wake me up magic! I was up way too late last night."

They smiled. "I'm done out there, what do you need in here?"

"I think we need more vanilla cupcakes. People tend to like them decorated for the 4th, those and chocolate. We make basic boxes to sell. You know, to compete with the grocery stores."

"That makes sense." Wes got out the recipe book, and started to page through it.

The door chimed and Wes dashed off. "Welcome to—"

"I don't need a welcome, Weslee White!" Dad's voice boomed out. "I work here. And if you don't recognize your seventh grade teacher, then I don't know what this world's coming to."

There was a squeal, almost as impressive as the girls', and a grunt. I could just imagine Wes giving Dad a hug. "Mr. Roads, it's so great to see you, can I get you anything? A cupcake? A cookie? Coffee?"

Dad scoffed. "Boy! You know I work here, don't you?" Laughter floated in and I smiled. "I'm just glad Rosy hired another guy. There are so many females around here," Dad's voice lowered, but not to the point I couldn't hear him, "you don't know what I've suffered!"

Wes chuckled. "It's great to see you Mr.—"

"And don't call me Mr. Roads. I have too many names around here. You can call me Gramps or Mitch. If I can get used to calling you Wes, you can adjust to a new name for me." There was a finality to Dad's words.

The two walked into the kitchen and they each started working on different cupcakes. Once Wes finished with their batch, they turned to me and asked, "What do I do now?"

They looked lost. For two days they'd been doing Dad's baking, and now he was here.

Dad guffawed. "You do the decorating." His hand waved towards the piping bags. "I thought that's what Rosy hired you for! Finally letting me focus on what I'm good at and off the hook for all that 'pretty' stuff."

The truth was, he'd taught me how to decorate. He was great at it, but he preferred baking.

When the first customer arrived, both Wes and Dad were a mess. "Got it."

Nikki sauntered in from across the street. I greeted her with a wave. "Hiya stranger. You don't come here that often. What can I get you?"

"Our coffee maker broke this morning and Nita and I are not doing well. I figure we need a couple of cookies and cupcakes to help put us in a good mood, as well as the coffees." Tired, her southern accent was thicker than normal. It amused me to hear it in our Midwestern town.

She pointed and I boxed up her order. "I can't imagine getting this far without the magic go-go juice."

"It was hard, but when you love your shop of horrors, it helps." She handed me some cash and waved off the change. "Speaking of horrors, did you see the old doll shop, with those antique terrors, has finally been bought? I swear they were possessed and would move around at night. Their eyes followed you when you walked past the store, it was freaky!"

A shiver ran down my spine. "That place was horrible. Do you remember when we were teens, and the owner changed the display every day for a month, moving those damn things around?"

"I tell you, Mrs. Paxton wasn't moving them, the damn dolls were moving themselves. They were possessed."

In the back I heard a small intake of breath and Dad's chuckles. It was his amusement of the dolls that kept me from being terrified.

Nikki shrugged. "Anyway, there's a sign, 'Coming Soon, Fun In The Sun Ice Cream'" She narrowed her eyes when I didn't react. "Do you know anything about this, Cookie Lady?"

"Maybe, but I don't know if the news is being spread. Once I have the thumbs up, I'll make sure you're the first on the block to know. Of course, once you know, everyone will know."

Her face scrunched up as she glared, but then it morphed into a laugh. "Fair enough. Until you have news to share." She headed out with her coffee and treats.

There was a rush of customers for the next hour. Wes and I took turns covering the front of the store, depending on who was able to run to the counter more easily.

"Morning Callen, I haven't seen you in awhile. How goes it?"

He looked happy, much less stressed than the last time he came in. "I'm good, really good. I can't believe how much my life has changed in the last few weeks. My job is perfect. Cindy has been amazing at helping me adjust—both to the library and life in Pekara. And living with Melody, Latina, and Franco ... I don't know, it's been great. I had no idea there were places like this and people lived this way."

"So you've embraced the poly-lifestyle?" I boxed up the items he indicated as we spoke.

He took a slow breath. "Yeah, I have. At first I was so confused about everything. I felt like I'd been dropped into an alternative universe. I kind of feel like I have, to be honest. But, I like it here." He huffed out a laugh and paid.

As he walked out, Cindy came in, eyeing the box. "Are those for the meeting in an hour?"

Callen paused. His order had been enough for a staff meeting, more than Melody ever gets for home. "I guess you'll have to be on time for once to find out." He took a step and stopped. "And Tim said eight coffees, not seven."

Cindy shook her head. "Why didn't he just send one of us?"

"Too much to carry?" Callen offered, then left before Cindy could gripe at him more.

As Cindy walked up, I began gathering coffee cups. "So, Ms. Fluffy Sugar Buns, anything besides the eight coffees for work?"

"Yes, I want a cookie, and why the name?"

"Because, have you figured out that damn cat's name yet? Maybe Sugar Buns?"

Cindy sighed. "Yes and no. I finally broke down and asked Selena because she wanted that damn collar for the cat. Well, she looked at me like I'd grown fricken horns. So I asked, what? She said, my cat? I thought the damn thing was your cat. Apparently, she kept waiting for *me* to call it by a consistent name. That's why she wanted a collar with a name."

I felt the kind of uncontrollable laughter coming from a ridiculous story, a good friend, and lack of sleep. "Okay, so what are you naming this beast?"

"I debated Stowaway, because she obviously ran in on move-in day. But Selena vetoed that name. We're going to go with Freckles."

"Why Freckles?"

"Because she has them on her face and butt, where she has a white patch."

I laughed harder. "Okay, anything else?" She handed me her work credit card for the coffees.

"How about you tell me about what happened last night? You never called. Did you even tell Mitch?"

"Tell me what?" His voice boomed out from the back.

Before I could open my mouth to answer, before I could even think, Cindy smirked and said, "Sacia is the real twin from the bus crash twelve years ago, not Charlie and Pris. We met her sister yesterday."

In an instant, Dad was next to me. "What?" His voice was crisp and sharp. "Where is she now? I didn't take her to camp, did you?" He asked Cindy.

"No, I assumed she went with the twins." She shook her head. "You know, the original twins."

"Stop." I held up my hands. "Yes, Sacia has a twin sister. Her name is Gilly."

"God, they both have weird names." Dad snorted.

"Dad! Stop."

"Fine, go on."

"Gilly is," I paused, knowing he wouldn't like this. "She's Elenora Shifer's daughter."

"What!?" Dad boomed. "Is that why she's here? Is that the real reason she chose this town?"

For a moment I wavered. *Could he be right? Was she here to steal my daughter away? Had she somehow figured it all out?*

"No, that's not it. I'm sure of it. The girls met at camp, and Nora was just as gobsmacked as me when she found out."

Dad's face softened. "Rosy, I love you like a daughter." I rolled my eyes at the old joke. "But you can be naive sometimes. She could've been acting."

"I don't think so."

Cindy slowly turned to me. "Who took Sacia to camp this morning?"

"Nora. She had a sleepover with Gilly last night."

Dad's face morphed and his head shook. "I can't believe how gullible you are. I'm going to that camp now, and if she isn't there, I'm going to the cops. Do you hear me?"

Terror washed through me, much stronger than any walking doll. "You're making something out of nothing Dad. She'll be at the camp. It's fine."

"I'm going."

A cross between dread and anger sent chills through me at the thought of my bullheaded Dad crashing through camp to find Sacia. "Wait." He stopped at the door. "Could we start with calling? I do have a number in case we need to get a hold of a camper. There's also Sacia's cell, you know. I understand you're getting on in age, but you know these things."

He stood by the door glaring as I called the camp. I put my phone on speaker. "Hello, Sonya speaking."

"Hi Sonya, this is Rosy, Sacia Roads's mom. Is Sacia there?"

"Hold on a moment." There was the sound of paper ruffling in the background. "It looks like she checked in. Do you need to speak with her?"

"No, that's fine. She spent the night at a friend's house and I hadn't heard from her this morning."

"Perfect. We'll see you at pick up."

"Thank you, Sonya."

Dad still looked angry. "Fine, but I still think you're too trusting."

Cindy took her items and mouthed, "Later."

As she left, Nora walked in. "Am I interrupting something?"

Dad narrowed his eyes at her, mumbled, "No." then headed to the back.

"How were the girls last night?"

Nora huffed out a humorless laugh. "Loud, but happy. They got to camp and the counselors seemed confused."

"Eh, it's probably good for them."

"I was just wondering if you wanted to go to the campground fireworks with me and Gilly tomorrow night. I hear the display is amazing." She smiled.

From the back, I heard Dad's grunt, but it sounded more positive than negative this time.

"Yeah, I would." My gut twisted with nerves, but I was so excited to have a date.

Nora smiled. "Great. I have a meeting. Maybe I'll text you later?"

"I'd like that." I knew I'd be like a teenager by my phone, staring at it until that text came.

Chapter 27 — A Bit Of History

Gilly

Sacia gave me a hug as Mom drove up. "Remember, ask about tomorrow and this weekend. I don't want to wait until forever to see you again."

"I know!" I pulled back and smiled. "I don't either. We have to spend as much time together this summer as we can. By the end, I want to know everything about you *and* the twins. We can become double double trouble!"

Behind her, Charlie and Pris laughed. Pris said, "You know it!"

Charlie added, "I can't wait for you to come spend time at our place. The four of us will have so much fun!"

She didn't say 'could' she said 'will'. These friends were just sure of my place with them. They'd never kick me to the curb for spending a summer away, they'd text me every day and ask me how I was. These three were true friends, sisters even.

I ran to the car and jumped in before they saw me tear up. There was no way for me to know if they truly felt as close to me as I was feeling towards them, but even though it'd only been a short amount of time, I couldn't imagine having better friends.

My nose smudged the window as I watched the world pass by. Mom knew me too well to not see I was feeling big feels.

"When were you born?"

"April second, why?"

"Wait, that's not a good question, is it, the two of you are twins. Actually all four of you have the same birthday. Gah!"

I laughed at Mom's frustration.

"Okay, what was the name of your second grade teacher?"

"Mom!"

"No? How about your first au pair?'

"Ma'oom!"

"What is your favorite thing to cook?"

"Ma'ooom!"

She laughed. "Okay, it's you, I'm certain of it."

Turning to face her, I joined in, laughing. "Oh? And what makes you so sure? I didn't answer one question."

"I disagree, you reacted to all of them. I know that 'Mom' yell anywhere. It's music to my ears."

"Ma'ooom!" I rolled my eyes.

"Well, maybe not music. But for now it lets me know I have the right Gilly."

"You could just look at my clothes, you know."

She rubbed the back of her neck. "Right, because that worked out well yesterday."

"Oh, right."

As we drove, she shot a quick look my way before concentrating on the road again. "We could dye a purple stripe down one side of your hair."

"No," I answered right away, then thought about it, my mind buzzing with new possibilities.

"Wait, what? Really? You'd let me dye my hair?" I'd always wanted to dye my hair. I didn't think she'd ever say yes.

Mom shook her head. "Probably not." My heart deflated. "But maybe your nails? Or maybe I could convince you or Sacia to get a buzz cut. Eventually you'll grow your hair out again, right?"

"Maybe." I shrugged. I found I rather liked the shorter hair. It was easier to take care of.

We turned away from the house. "Where are we going?" I swung my head back and forth.

"To the local museum." She made another turn. "Would your coach frown on colored hair? Is it against track rules or something?"

Excitement built within me. Was she changing her mind? "No. There are a few girls on the team who've dyed their hair. No one seems to mind."

"Huh. Do you like the idea of a purple stripe?" "Probably blue. Maybe two." I started vibrating in my seat. "I know just the right style. I can find images online to show you. You are the coolest mom ever!"

"We can discuss this further when we get to a store that sells hair dye. But the next question is who will dye it? I've never done this."

I scrunched up my face, then decided in for a penny and all that. "I've talked to Delia about it a few times. I think she could do it."

"Delia? Okay, we can ask her, but no pestering. If she says 'No,' we'll ask Rosy if she knows anyone in town she'd trust."

My mind nearly exploded over this conversation. Was Mom genuinely offering to have my hair dyed? I couldn't believe it. "Okay, whatever you say."

She smirked as we pulled into the lot.

I looked around. This location was new and really pretty. I started to bounce when I saw Delia standing at the door. "Delia's here! You never told me." When the car stopped, I lightly slapped Mom's arm, then leapt out, running to give Delia a hug.

"Hiya Gilly, you seem in a good mood."

"Did you hear? Did Mom tell you?"

Delia's gaze jumped up to Mom and back to me. "Honestly, I've been holed up with my family. I'm very much out of the loop."

"But you're from here, you had to have known about the bakery and the other bus kids."

"Gilly, medical school lasts for six years, high school four. If you do the math, that bus crashed when I was twelve, your age actually. Though I knew something was going on, I never knew much."

"So you didn't know that three of the kids lived in town?"

She gazed up towards the clouds. "You do know that I don't often think of you as being one of the bus kids, right. You're just the kid that I take care of."

"Oh, right. I guess that isn't a big part of my life. You started caring for me, like, five years ago. By then the bus wasn't that big of a thing anymore."

"Nope." She tapped my nose. "So, even though I did know there were bus crash kids here, I never made the connection that you may want to meet people from my town."

"Do you know Rosy and her daughter Sacia?"

"Not that well. I mean, I've been in the bakery, but not that often."

"Here, look at this picture of me and the bakery owner's daughter." I pushed my phone to Delia, who took it.

"Whoa, you two—" She looked at Mom.

"Yeah, I know. They have to be the real twins from the accident. There had to have been a mix up with all the confusion and chaos."

"That's ... I don't know what it is." She handed my phone back to me. "Is Sacia nice?"

"She's the best."

Delia smiled. "I'm glad." She reached over to take my hand. "I wanted you to see a bit of the history of my town. I hope that's okay."

"Sure, that sounds great." We followed her in.

There were all sorts of pictures and statues as well as artifacts depicting not only Pekara but this part of Wisconsin. As we walked, I read plaques and studied original outfits. I was excited and wanted to talk with Sacia to see how much of this she knew about.

"Come check this out. It is part of the more recent history of Pekara."

Delia led me into a small room. She seemed very excited to share whatever was hidden within.

The room had a few banners and pendants with what I realized was the school's name on it. As I looked around, there were trophies and awards to students who had won national awards in athletics and academics. "Wow, students from Pekara have been doing some pretty solid things for years."

"Yep, my sister went to the Science Olympiad Nationals her sophomore and senior years and they brought home medals and recognitions. My brothers went to DC for Deca. The school pushes both the mind and the body."

There were so many students who had been recognized, chills ran down my spine. Then I saw it and froze. "Delia! Mom! Look at this! There is a section for people who have both tried out and have gone to the Olympics. There have been people who have gone in several different disciplines, but there have been people, living in *this* town, who have medaled in running and other track and field events in the Olympics. The Olympics! You said went, not medaled."

"Yep. There is a pretty competitive sports program here." Delia said. "There are a few tracks, one is for your every day student, but they have honors track, so to speak, for students who genuinely want to train and train hard."

Everything in my body froze and tingles raced up and down my arms and legs. I couldn't believe what I was hearing. "Why didn't you tell me this before?"

"To what end? You live in Milwaukee, sweetest Gilly."

I wanted to snarl. "Then why show me now? It's like you're trying to tease me."

"Honestly? Because my Dad suggested I take you here. He's friends with the coach and said that if we're planning on spending the rest of the summer here, you could train with the runners one or two days a week. Before I made the offer, I wanted to show you that training here wouldn't be beneath you."

I turned so quickly I almost lost my balance. "Mom, can I? Please?"

"What about camp? Your new friends?"

"What about them? They're my friends. They'll be excited for me. That's what good friends do. They don't drop you or be awful."

Her smile lit up her face. "I'm glad you know that. Okay, on Monday I'll go with Delia to see what can be arranged since everything is closed tomorrow."

As much as I wanted an immediate answer, I knew that this was as good as it got. "Thank you!

Oh, and do you think we could spend the 4th with Sacia and the twins at the park? And maybe I could spend the night with the twins some time?"

Delia gaped at me, looking confused. "The twins?"

We explained as we continued to tour the museum. Everything I told her made me more and more happy.

Chapter 28 — A Walk In The Park

Nora

My morning coffee steamed as I sipped it, savoring the taste. Gilly was growing up too fast. Already twelve, she wanted to spend the night away, had plans to dye her hair, and do all sorts of things I felt were far too old for her young age. All that said, the fact that she slept past six wasn't anything I complained about. I figured the difficulties of waking her up in a few years would be a headache, but for now, mornings were a nice balance.

I debated a second cup when the twelve-year-old herself exploded out from her room, zooming around the kitchen, putting any cat to shame. "Mom, I got a text from Sacia, she and the twins are at the bakery making something, I don't know what, I don't understand baking words, but they invited me to come watch. Can I go?"

The words had come at me so fast, I worried for her tongue at times. Rubbing my temples, I worried for my head. "Just you? Or both of us?"

"I don't think they care if you come or don't. I mean, I was invited, but you and Rosy are also friends, right? Like she doesn't hate you or anything, or does she? Have you been mean to her?"

Two minutes. That was all it took, and I wanted to take a nap. "Let me go get some clean clothes on and we can head to Main Street. If Rosy or Mitch don't want us bothering them, we're leaving."

"Fi-ine!" She spun and headed to her room.

I no longer knew what I had thought was easy about this age.

When we entered, a new person waved at us from the counter. "Welcome, how can we help you?" Then their eyes narrowed. "Wait, I know you. You're Sacia's doppelganger. The one that tried to fool Rosy, but failed."

Gilly laughed. "That's right. And this is my mom."

"Well hello, Mom. I'm Wes."

"I'm Nora. Nice to meet you."

There was a stampede. I debated ducking and covering, but they reached us before I could decide. Then Gilly was part of the horde, and they were off.

At the counter, Wes smiled. "Well, that's one way to become one with the youth. Can I get you a coffee?"

"Yes, please."

Rosy stuck her head out. "I would offer to take a walk or something, but Dad may kill me for leaving him with four of them."

"Go! If I can deal with a class of hellions, I can manage these four, even when two of them are pretending to be the same tween." Mitch narrowed his eyes. "Would the two of you mind if I take a sharpie and draw something on the back of each of their hands?"

Rosy snorted. "If you can convince Sacia, go for it."

I shrugged. "Same answer."

Dad's face brightened. "I was kind of joking, didn't expect a positive response. Forgot for a moment I wasn't actually in a classroom. Maybe I can do something for all four of them, that way they all feel involved." One of his brows rose as he trudged back to the kitchen in thought.

Wes waved their hands in a shooing motions. "You heard the man, go. I for one don't want to get on his bad side."

Rosy grumbled low, but took off her apron. "Fine, kick me out of my own establishment. I know when I'm not wanted."

Peals of laughter followed us out.

I linked my arm in hers. "I didn't actually expect to have any time with you."

"Me either. I didn't expect to see you until tomorrow. How are you doing today?" Walking down the street, I realized this was the most relaxed I'd seen Rosy. It was a nice look on her.

"Oh, you know. My daughter is a twin, and while I'm spiraling, she's loving every second of it. Beyond that, I think she's fallen in love with this town."

Rosy bumped shoulders with me. "Why not? It's an amazing place."

"But our home, our life, is in Milwaukee."

"I get it. I've traveled a lot, and bigger cities are exciting and just, I don't know, more I guess. If I were used to living with public transportation and easy access to everything, I don't know if I'd want to downsize." We walked for a few steps before she asked, "Do you have family there? A big friend group?"

As we walked, Rosy slowly guided us towards a park with a path that led through the center of the manicured lawn, plots of vibrant flowers, and established trees. "Right now, it's just me and Gilly in Milwaukee. I'm originally from just south of Madison, a small town. I moved to Milwaukee for college, but most of the people I knew back then have left."

We passed a woman on the path who smiled and waved. "Rosy, you're not in the bakery. It's nice to see you out and about."

"Tonya! Where's Reggie?" She tilted her head towards me. "They come regularly for her work's staff meeting. She always gets her son something."

"He's home with Dad playing video games."

I smiled. "Sounds fun."

She narrowed her eyes. "Don't forget what I told you. You should expand. You're too popular a shop to not have a second location."

"Alright, I'm thinking about it."

As the other woman walked away, I squeezed Rosy's arm. "You are?"

"Eh? I don't know. Whenever I imagine opening up more locations, my mind short circuits and I have to turn on the TV and watch some show I've recorded."

I laughed. "Well, I wouldn't want to ruin your TV stories. That said, if you do decide to expand, I could always help."

"Wouldn't that be a conflict of interest?"

"No, because I'm interested in you, oh tempting one." A tremour passed through her body and she sighed.

"I do like the sound of that, though I keep reminding myself this ends in a few weeks when you head back to Milwaukee."

Down the path, an older man approached, jogging. Rosy waved. "Dylan, you look so different in shorts and a tank top! I would figure you exercised in a suit."

He chuckled as he approached. "Rosy! You have a bottom half! Nice to see you out of the bakery enjoying life."

"How are you? Did you figure out your skunk problem?"

He stopped by us, jogging in place. I couldn't imagine what she meant by a skunk problem. "Yes, the cameras worked perfectly. My guess had been correct, Leigh had been so annoyed about the no perfume or scented lotion rule that she'd come in early and spray her perfume up and down the executive hallway and throughout the shop. She even spread some lotions onto the carpets."

I couldn't believe what I heard, and Rosy's mouth dropped open. She leaned forward. "No way! Every morning?"

"Yep. She would come in early to make coffee and bring bagels or treats."

Rosy's face contorted. "She never came to the bakery to buy anything."

The man—*Did Rosy say Dylan?*—laughed. "No, she was never known for having good taste. She'd buy stuff from the closest gas station to her house. It was often the day old stuff on sale, stale and hard. It was always awful. Half the stuff would end up in the garbage, and you know my people, they'll eat just about anything."

"So what did you do?"

"What I probably should've done months if not years ago. I fired her. I'll be looking for someone new starting next week, but to be honest, anyone will be better than her." He looked at his watch. "Oh! Gotta run, literally."

"See ya, Dylan."

"Bye Rosy, see you Monday with something new, I'm sure."

Her face lit up. "Looking forward to it!"

And he was off.

A few more people passed by with a tid bit of gossip or a word or two of encouragement that Rosy was finally out and about relaxing.

In the center of the park was a bench, and I forced Rosy to sit. "My goodness, everyone in the town knows you. You're like gossip central."

"I am!" She laughed. "I love it, too. I won't lie. It's fun having everyone tell me everything. I'm the morning barkeep."

The day was beautiful with trees so full of leaves they looked ready to burst. Birds sang songs and a breeze ruffled the grass and bushes, spreading the sweet scent of the flowers.

A part of me wanted to wrap Rosy and Sacia up and bring them home with me to Milwaukee. Let the girls be sisters and Rosy be ... something. We'd figure that out as we went along. But I couldn't see her leaving the town. She was as much a part of it as any other fixture.

She leaned into me. "Do you ever watch TV?"

The simplicity of the question amused me. "Of course I do."

"Any guilty pleasures?"

"Besides this?" I stretched my arm over her shoulder and she leaned in. I loved how well she fit.

"Yes. Television shows, silly." Despite the words, she sounded content.

"I could tell you, but then I'd have to kill you." She tried to pull away with an indignant sound, but I held tight. There wasn't much fight before she settled back down.

"Fine, you can be that way, but I'll tell you." She shifted and settled a bit closer to me. "I've been watching *Playing It Queer.*"

"I'll admit, I'd love to be all judgy, but since I know one of the women on the show, I've been watching it too."

Her head tilted up so she could look at me. "Wait, you what?" She almost sounded angry.

"We can discuss that on a later date." My arm tightened, trying to extend our cuddle, but Rosy pushed away, staring at me as if she wanted to read my mind.

She leaned in a bit and her head tilted. "Is she the one who is straight?"

A laugh bubbled from me. "I don't know. She's my niece, but we're not that close."

"Your what?" Rosy gaped, eyes the size of saucers. "Your niece is on the show and you don't know if she's straight? When was the last time you spoke to her? To her parents?"

"Oh no. You're not pulling me into one of these drama filled discussions. If we ever end up in front of a TV when the show's on, then we can discuss all of this, otherwise, it can wait."

"Fine." Her finger dug into my shoulder. "But I expect this to happen before you disappear to Milwaukee, pretty lady."

For some reason, every time Rosy mentioned our spending time together being short term, something within me hurt.

Chapter 29 — An Explosive Evening

Rosy

The girls ran to one of the people all aglow with bracelets, crowns, necklaces, and other do-dads that would glow for the remainder of the evening. Leaning back on my arms, legs stretched out, I let the last remnants of the sun soak into me. The park had some space now, but in the next few hours it would be a zoo, packed with more people than could possibly live anywhere near Pekara. For the time being I wanted to enjoy the few moments of perceived peace.

"Mom, mom, mom, mom, *mom!*"

With effort, I cracked one of my eyes open to watch as Sacia barreled towards me with Pris and Charlie. "What, what, what, what, *what?*"

"Should we get something for Gilly? When is she going to get here? Have you called her mom?" She stood a few feet away, bouncing on her toes.

"Don't you have her cell phone number? Can't *you* call, or, more likely text?" My eyes narrowed. "What do you know of calling people anyway? Isn't that anathema to people your age?"

"Mom!"

"Sacia!"

Behind her Pris smirked and Charlie laughed.

I pushed up and gazed at them. "I think you three should get what you want and if and when Gilly shows up, you can help her pick something out. Don't you think she should decide for herself what she wants?"

"But what if she wants to match me and they're all sold out?"

Behind the girls, I saw Nora and Gilly weaving their way through the crowd. Their heads swung back and forth looking for us. *Does Gilly have a blue hair clip or two in her hair?*

One side of my mouth twitching, I tried to keep a poker face, but I knew I failed. "You'll just have to chance it. Now go, or I'll change my mind about you getting that glowing bounty."

Sacia made a disapproving pre-teen face. I was a bit surprised and, to be honest, disappointed when she didn't stomp or do some physical show of her anger, before turning and seeing Gilly. Then she hopped and squealed. *God, my poor ears.* "Gilly!" And then the three were off.

The three swarmed Nora, whose hands lifted to the air as she watched the gaggle of girls. Then she pulled out her wallet, gave Gilly some money, and the four fled.

Nora flopped down next to me. She looked so relaxed in jeans and a button-down. I took a moment to appreciate her beauty even when dressed casually. Then I found the girls in the slowly growing crowd. "Did I see blue in Gilly's hair?"

"You did. We dyed it so she couldn't swap places with Sacia again, it was that or try to convince you to buzz cut your daughter's head."

"Oh, I'm betting that wouldn't have caused any issues." Sarcasm dripped from my words, rivaling even my daughter.

Nora bumped her shoulder to mine. "Probably not. Twelve-year-old girls are known for their level headedness."

The noise let us know the girls were back. "Mom! I want to color my hair, too! Look at Gilly, it's sooooo ... I don't know. Can I?"

With a grunt, I finally pushed myself up to sitting. "The point is to be able to tell you two apart."

"Not blue. Maybe green and gold. Then I could be the school's colors."

"Or pink and purple and you could look like one of Gramps cupcakes." I winked as the others chuckled.

Sacia rolled her eyes. "Is that a yes, then? Can we look for colors tomorrow?"

Both Charlie and Pris surrounded her, speaking softly. All three whispered, their heads nodding and bobbing. After a moment, Gilly joined them, adding a word or two.

Once the four separated, almost in perfect synchrony, they formed a line with Sacia and Gilly in the center. Twins surrounded by twins. I wasn't sure if I should laugh or find them matching outfits. Sacia's eyes twinkled in a tell, which meant she was up to no good. "Mom, Ms. Shifer—"

"Nora, sweety. Call me Nora."

"Right, Nora." She gave a single curt nod, took in a deep breath, then smiled wide. *God above, I was in for a rough few years.* "Mom, Nora, the four of us would like to find Pris and Charlie's parents. They texted a few minutes ago that not only are they here, but they both have tomorrow off. If they're okay with it, can both me and Gilly spend the night?"

"So, no dying your hair, that works for me." I smirked and she sneered.

"That can happen later."

Nora looked at the four girls, then at me. "I'd like to meet the parents first, make sure they're okay with having so many more kids over. We're talking about doubling what they're used to."

Charlie pulled out her phone and Pris's head bobbed left and right. "Not really. Sacia stays over a lot. It's just going from three to four. That's barely an increase at all, if you think about it."

"They're almost here. I told them where to find us." Charlie's smile spread to all the girls and my heart warmed.

This group of kids was amazing.

"My god, Sacia went and replicated herself! There's two of her." Sammi's voice came from behind me as she and Lucas arrived and set up next to us.

"Mom! Dad!" Both Charlie and Pris ran over to help.

I stood to make introductions. Then I asked, "Did you know your kids were offering up your house for this swarm for tonight?"

Lucas laughed. "We did. I think it'd be a hoot to have all four of them tomorrow. We actually were thinking of, he leaned in, blocking his mouth from the kids, "heading to Great America, if that was okay with you two."

Nora's eyes widened, but I just nodded. "They've been asking for weeks."

"I know." Lucas said. "I finally got the time off. Two days including today. I'm not sure how it happened, but I want to goof off for once!"

"Are you sure?" Nora sounded dumbfounded.

"Absolutely. Look at them. They'll practically take care of themselves."

I couldn't figure out the look or emotion that passed over Nora's face. The four of us sat on the blanket I'd brought and gave the Weber's over to the girls. We had food and drink, and waited for dark and the start of the fireworks.

When the first explosion lit up the sky, a blue ball that ended in white sparkles, Nora leaned over and kissed me. The fireworks within my body were more impressive than anything in the sky.

With the display above and the cheering all around, I didn't have to worry about covering up my moans of desire.

After a few minutes in which I wasn't sure if the snapping sounds were in the sky or my body's reaction to the woman hovering above me, Nora pulled away. "If we weren't in a field, surrounded by so many people, including our daughters ..." Her forehead landed on mine.

I laughed humorlessly. "Agreed." I let my hand drop from her arm where I'd been enjoying the feel of its strength.

"You have such a great town here with amazing people. Do you understand how lucky you and Sacia are?" There was desperation in her voice.

Gazing into her eyes, I lifted my hand to wrap behind her neck. "You do know, the town isn't closed to newcomers, right?"

"But my life is in Milwaukee."

A bit of me chilled at her words. "I know. But we can enjoy tonight."

"We can, but maybe after the fireworks ..."

"Hmm." I hummed. "I get two firework displays?"

She laughed.

Chapter 30 — Cookies And Pie

Nora

The kitchen at Road's Café And Bakery was large, clean, and inviting. I spent so little time in industrial kitchens these days that I forgot how much I loved being in one.

We arrived at a stupid early hour. I didn't miss that, though I still tended to wake early. Rosy had told me to go back to sleep, but I decided to follow her. Her voluptuous movements did things to me, and watching her, especially watching her bake, wasn't worth missing.

As she held a tray of Snickerdoodles, turning to put them in an oven, I realized I could watch her do this every morning. She was worth losing sleep over.

Holy shit, when the hell did I fall in love with her. Am I in love with her? This can't work, I live in Milwaukee, my life is there, Gilly's life is there. There's no way we could make something long distance work.

"I still don't know why you're not cozy in a warm bed. You must be bored out of your mind. You kind of look like you're in a daze." Rosy smiled at me, shaking her head.

"No, I just forgot the feeling of being in a kitchen this early. It's been awhile."

She smirked. "And if you were to join me ... um, in baking right now. What would you bake?"

Is she thinking about more than just baking? Does Rosy want something more long term as well?

One of my brows rose in challenge. "I mean, you do know what I named my bakeries, right?"

She laughed out a bark. "Are you pulling my leg? Pies? That's what you'd bake?"

"Says the woman who only bakes cookies."

"Hey! I bake other things. Do you know how many cakes I've made? I can even make them into funky shapes."

Both my brows rose this time. "Like round or square?"

Rosy snorted. "I made one in the shape of a dog for Charlie's birthday and a unicorn for Pris's birthday. Thank you very much Ms. Skeptical."

"Their birthdays' are on the same day. What did Sacia get that year?"

"An ice cream cake, thank goodness. I think three novelty cakes at once would've killed me."

Amusement lifted my spirits, and I laughed. For the first time I really thought about Rosy and the twins' parents raising the three together. As much as they entertained themselves, I couldn't imagine the times she had to do things with all of them together.

I let my eyes roam the kitchen, again feeling the peace of the space. "This kitchen is lovely ... especially being here with you." I got up, seeing she was between batches, and wrapped her in a hug.

She made a protesting sound, but physically didn't resist. The kiss I instigated was just as soul shattering as all the others. This woman did things to me no one else had ever done, and I was fully addicted to her.

Pushing away with a laugh, she said, "You're going to mess up your outfit, and I need to make the next batch."

"What if I don't want to let you go ... ever."

Rosy stilled in my arms, gazing into my eyes. I'm not sure what she saw, but her hands slid up my arms to behind my neck. "I don't want to let you go either, Nora, I haven't in a long time. If I had my way, I'd keep you here, in Pekara, both you and Gilly. Ever since the night in the bar, I can't stop thinking about you."

"Even when you hated me?"

Her smile lit her face and I wanted to melt into her the way we'd done the night before. Everything about this woman was perfect. "That's just it. I had to work to hate you. Fight my instinct and body's every desire. If I were to be honest, which I know is probably dumb," she bit her lip as if debating, "I probably fell in love with you weeks ago despite believing I should hate you."

I squeezed her tighter, my body electrified by her words. *How could this actually be happening? How can I be this lucky?*

Resting my forehead on hers, I said, my voice husky, "I love you, Rosy Roads."

"I love you, too, Nora Shifer."

Chapter 31 — Friends Are Sisters And Sisters Are Friends

Sacia

Though a few people from school went to camp with us, most of the middle schoolers gaped as Gilly and I walked through the halls arm in arm.

"I know why our moms wanted us to have different color streaks in our hair, but this would've been so much more fun if we could've come today looking exactly the same."

Gilly chuckled and I felt her relax. On Gilly's far side, Pris snorted. "All four of us should've dressed in matching shirts, then when someone said stupidly, 'You two look alike.', Charlie or I could've said, 'Duh! We're twins.' Then we could let the idiot sputter."

All four of us laughed.

This may be a new school for Gilly, but she already had her people, and that was half the battle. Mom and coach also made sure she and I were in the same homeroom. The fact that Pris and Charlie were in that class as well was just frosting on the cupcake.

When we left, we promised Lucas, who dropped us off, that we'd not misbehave. We knew better than to disrupt class and be separated to the four corners.

Gilly looked at a piece of paper. "Okay, so this building is a lot bigger than I thought it would be for a backwards, farm loving, middle school."

"Hey, now!" My jaw dropped and I punched her in the arm.

She laughed, blew a raspberry, then continued. "Coach said, during the last period of the day, when you have gym, I should get into a car that will take me to the high school for track. That will be," she stopped and spun, then pointed. "Over there, right?"

Pris took her by the shoulders and rotated her a quarter of a turn. "That way. One of us can lead you around, don't worry. The teachers around here are pretty relaxed about that during the first week. They'll know you're new ... assuming they don't think you're Sacia."

She nodded, her eyes getting bigger. *Is that what I look like when I'm confused?* I tried not to laugh.

Charlie smirked, "The big question becomes, do we go to the bakery after school or the ice cream shop. We now have two skills to master."

Eyes twinkling, Gilly shook her head. "Nope, not even ice cream will get me to love kitchen-ing. Just tell me which location, or I'll check them both out. Watching you three mess about is plenty fun. And I can judge your final products."

When we got to the classroom, the teacher, Mrs. Gilbert, narrowed her eyes. "Okay, I've been warned about you lot. A lot about you lot!" She chuckled at her own joke. "Gilly?" Her eyes bounced between me and my soon to be official sister ... at least I was hoping it would become official.

Gilly raised her hand. Mrs. Gilbert wrote something down on her clipboard. "Okay, I know you're new to town. Choose one of the others to sit next to you, the other two have to have some space between the others. No easy access to talking. Do this voluntarily, or I'll assign seats."

The pressure on our linked arms tightened, and Gilly dragged me to the far side seats by the window, a couple of rows back. Pris sat front row center and Charlie sat front row corner, two seats in front of Gilly.

Not only were we separated, we were close to where we could be monitored. We all wanted to learn and not get caught in middle school drama.

For years we'd been the triplets. Everyone in school knew that. As I gazed at my friends, my people, my sisters, a warmth built in me. I'd always felt connected to the twins. I wondered if it was because I knew I had a twin of my own out there, someone I just had to find.

Well, now she was here, and this town had better be ready for all of us!

Musing From The Author

This book is a fun little romance written in the Hallmark style. When I started this, I had a few plans. I wanted a conflict between the two main characters, enemies to lovers. I'd just listened to a Parent Trap type book, and barely into the story, the way the author handled it ... I was annoyed. I decided, that's it! I'm doing it better. Many of the names of the characters are of people I know. The relationships may not be correct for the people, but writing this book has warmed my heart as I've thought of many people who are dear to me.

The other books in the series will follow this trend.

Thank you for reading
Bakery Wars!

Please Leave a review for this book so others
know how much you enjoyed reading it.

Find more information on my books on my
website

About the Author

Harlowe Frost has been a teacher at both the high school and college level. Her parents instilled a love of reading from a young age. She grew up in the queer community. Her favorite genre growing up was fantasy and science fiction, that is, until she discovered urban fantasy and paranormal romance. What she never found in those books was the diversity in background, gender identity, and sexuality she saw in the people around her. She decided if she couldn't find that in what she read, then she would write it herself. This started her writing paranormal romance with a LGBTQ+ background.